MIDNIGHT DOORWAYS

Usman T. Malik is a Pakistani–American writer and doctor. His fiction has won the Bram Stoker Award and the British Fantasy Award. His work has been published in several anthologies, including the Best American Science Fiction and Fantasy series, and has been nominated for the World Fantasy Award, the Million Writers Award and twice for the Nebula. *Midnight Doorways: Stories* (first published in Pakistan as *Midnight Doorways: Fables from Pakistan*) is Usman's debut collection.

MIDNIGHT DOORWAYS

Stories

Usman T. Malik

hachette INDIA

First published in 2021 in Pakistan as *Midnight Doorways: Fables from Pakistan*
by Kitab (Pvt) Ltd.

This edition published in 2022 by Hachette India
(Registered name: Hachette Book Publishing India Pvt. Ltd)
An Hachette UK company
www.hachetteindia.com

ISBN 978-93-91028-93-0

For sale in India only.

Hachette Book Publishing India Pvt. Ltd
4th & 5th Floors, Corporate Centre
Plot No. 94, Sector 44, Gurugram 122003, India

Typeset in Adobe Caslon Pro 11/14.5
by R. Ajith Kumar, New Delhi

Printed and bound in India
by Manipal Technologies Limited, Manipal

FSC
www.fsc.org
MIX
Paper from
responsible sources
FSC® C043100

Praise for *Midnight Doorways*

'Under the gorgeous prose and vivid images lies a seductive and sinister magic; Malik is the spellcaster par excellence. Uneasy, unpredictable and unforgettable.'

— Karen Joy Fowler, Man Booker-nominated author of *We Are All Completely Beside Ourselves*

'Wielding a prose style at once dispassionate as ice and poignant as autumn, Malik invokes worlds of enchantment and magic superimposed over our sublunary realm: dangerous, lush, hopeful, seductive, defiant, mirrors into which we gaze to find our own truths.'

— Ken Liu, award-winning author of *The Paper Menagerie and Other Stories* and *The Grace of Kings*

'Mesmerizing and provocative, Malik's collection is not to be missed. Impossible to put down, achingly gorgeous, even as the tales dive into the deepest and most disturbing depths of both humanity and the ancient – and here, quite justified! – fear of the unknown.'

— S.A. Chakraborty, award-winning author of *The City of Brass*

'Some writers go a step past, into the darkness, but that step past is just a starting point for Usman T. Malik. But he'll call back for you. You can't see him, he's gone too far, but you can close your eyes, follow his voice. If you dare.'

— Stephen Graham Jones, award-winning author of *The Only Good Indian*s

'Rich, textured and beautifully written, these vivid stories can be disturbing and often horrific and yet they are grounded in a deep well of compassion for human frailty and loss.'

— Kate Elliott, *New York Times*' bestselling author of *Unconquerable Sun* and *Cold Magic*

'Brilliant writer, one to watch out for and buy everything instantly forever.'

— Jo Walton, Hugo, Nebula, and World Fantasy award-winning author of *Among Others*

'Literary horror at its finest. *Midnight Doorways* contains seven stories of painful beauty, by turns eerie, disturbing, heartbreaking and hideous. It's Malik at his best.'

— Christopher Golden, *New York Times'* bestselling author of *Ararat* and *Snowblind*

'Usman T. Malik is a major talent with a highly original voice, and this is a treasure house of his work. Viscerally vivid and luminously lyrical, his tales bring an entire country to life with an immediacy many veteran writers might envy. There is beauty and awe and the darkest horrors, both supernatural and social, all of which Malik unites into a rich unique blend. An essential book for every aficionado's shelf – haunting, challenging and often powerfully moving.'

— Ramsey Campbell, selected author, *Masters of the Weird Tale: Ramsey Campbell*

'Usman T. Malik's collection of stories *Midnight Doorways* is a pleasure to read and re-read. Though the stories are authentically rooted in the here and now, they infuse the mind with the subtle fragrance of the uncanny. This work is a standout addition to the literatures of the imagination.'

— Anil Menon, The Hindu Literary Prize–nominated author of *Half of What I Say*

'I love reading stories by Usman T. Malik because I always know that I'll be surprised and dazzled – whether he's weaving a tantalizing tale of love and loss or leading me down a dark, twisted road as he provides his unique take on Lovecraftian horror. You are so lucky, dear reader, to experience several of his stories in this debut collection.'

— Ellen Datlow, Hugo Award–winning editor of The Best Horror of the Year series

'Usman T. Malik is the jinn of storytellers. He weaves a magic that is both fresh and familiar, specific to Pakistan and universal, all at once. There's a ruthless honesty to his work, whether he's dealing with lovers, siblings, heroinichis, terrorists, orphans or ghosts.'

— Priya Sharma, Shirley Jackson Award–winning author of *Ormeshadow* and *All the Fabulous Beasts*

'A tremendous achievement. Written in prose of exquisite mellifluousness but also of great emotive power, this book offers us vivid facets of the sights, sounds and smells of Pakistan. Malik's tales, whether they are of dreamlike fantasy or clutching horror, evoke for us the little tragedies that have disfigured the lives of his characters; and yet, those characters still manage to find a vibrant wonder in the world they see around them. No devotee of supernatural literature, or of fine writing, can afford to miss this book.'

— S. T. Joshi, author of *I Am Providence: The Life and Times of H. P. Lovecraft.*

'Usman T. Malik's book-length collection is a much anticipated event in SFF circles. He is a gifted writer, traversing the realms of SF, fantasy and the Weird with rare grace and empathy. This volume of short stories includes the luminous and disturbing Resurrection Points. Malik's training as a physician produces stories which are both moving and thought-provoking. Indeed, he invites us to reflect anew on questions of secular transcendence in our modern world.'

— Tarun Saint, editor of *The Gollancz Book of South Asian Science Fiction*

'I am not a reader of horror fiction, but I always make an exception for the stories of Usman T. Malik. They plumb the depths of human experience, giving form to the worst nightmares within and outside us in prose that is at once precise and lyrical. Luminous, profound and terrifying, these stories illuminate and enrich the scope and reach of literary speculative fiction. A unique and compelling voice in the genre!'

— Vandana Singh, Philip K. Dick Award–nominated author of *Ambiguity Machines and Other Stories*

'Usman T. Malik is a master of short horror fiction – one of the best of his generation.'

— Brian Keene, World Horror Grandmaster and author of *The Rising*

'A phenomenal reading experience. I've never seen anything like these stories. Fiercely original and beautifully told, these worlds will linger with you long after you've turned the final page.'

— Ausma Zehanat Khan, author of *The Bloodprint*

'The best horror is made of contrasts. Usman T. Malik's prose is both searing and gentle, arcane yet conversational. His stories unwind like myths and lead you to that place where the shadows meet reality – stark, sometimes visceral and meaty, but always deeply, heartbreakingly humanistic.'

— Jennifer Giesbrecht, author of *The Monster of Elendhaven*

'Look no further than *Midnight Doorways* for confirmation that Usman T. Malik is one of the best writers of horror and dark fantasy working today. A beautiful and unsettling debut collection that feels distinctly South Asian in its exploration of how the mythic past and the broken present entangle and tear at each other in this part of the world.'

— Indrapramit Das, award-winning author of *The Devourer*

For my mother, and for Kiran.
They know why.

It was narrated from Jabir ibn Abd-Allah (may Allah be pleased with him) that the Prophet (peace and blessings of Allah be upon him) said:

'When the wings of the night open keep your children in, for the devils spread out at that time... And close the doors and mention the name of Allah, for Satan does not open a closed door. And tie up your waterskins and mention the name of Allah, and cover your vessels and mention the name of Allah... and extinguish your lamps.'

—Al-Bukhari,
The Book on the Beginning of Creation

'Their dread becomes wish: they yearn for what they fear.'

—Dante Alighieri,
The Inferno: Canto III

CONTENTS

ISHQ

They whispered: Parveen is in love with the shakarkandi vendor.

Figures, said the shocked neighbourhood women. Fitting, that the girl with polio, who stood at her window every night staring into the ghostly depth of Narrow Alley would steal glances at the bright-eyed boy with muscles, sharp and confident in his back and a smile on his lips. When Hashim went with his basket of steamed sweet potato up the alley, yodelling at the top of his voice, 'Shakarkandi-walla. Shakarkandi-walla' many a middle-aged lady sighed dreamily and leaned out of her window to watch him go. Come taste my wares, his lilting, young man's voice teased. Come take a bite of my sweet potatoes.

And they wanted to go. Wanted to take their drawstring purses, abandon the baby carriage in the hall with its shit-stained linen, abolish all principles of a vaguely understood domesticity and run screaming after the sing-song boy, 'Wait. Oh, please wait. One packet of your shakarkandi, please. Stay a moment, won't you? No, you're charging too much. Leave my alley now, you lying scumbag. But throw me over your shoulders and take me *with you.*'

Such sins that our daydreams are made of. The women watched the sweat of Hashim's labour trickle down the brown lobes of his exquisite ears, watched his bare chest shine with summer heat; and in the evening, they'd gather in the cool sprawling gardens near Mosque Wazir Khan and make fun of the boy. Who would ever go with *him*? they'd ask each other, wide-eyed, and laugh nervously. Who would go with this lanky, young, beautiful fool who never stopped grinning.

Seemly then that Parveen was the answer. The pale girl whose high, gloomy room looked down upon the alley from a dusty window. Every evening she leaned out, red and yellow bangles slipping down her willowy arms until they shone in the dark like jewels. They clinked above the din of the street *khanak! khanak!* a soul song borrowed from centuries of Punjabi lore, and the girl's eyes would be restless and lustreless until they riveted on the boy pedalling toward her house.

Hashim's route was fixed. Each morning he biked down the alley, navigating the narrowest points on foot. Come dusk, he walked his bicycle up, smiling, yelling to labourers and shopkeepers returning home to try his shakarkandi. He had a sweet, affecting voice, and when he was not hawking his merchandise he sang Sufi love verses that pealed in the night like bells: 'Everywhere I turn I see Ranjha; so long

I've chanted Ranjha Ranjha, I've become him myself. Call me Ranjha, sisters, don't call me Heer no more.'

Carefully he'd decorate his wicker basket with shakarkandi. Blossoms of sweet potato wedges sat skewered on toothpicks ringed with slices of lemon, a presentation to tempt the most jaded taste buds, and the people of Narrow Alley responded. They gathered around, waited for him to sprinkle chaat masala over their purchase, and munched the shakarkandi all the way home.

It was on one such night when the boy clattered down the alley, good-naturedly tinkling his bell at pedestrians that he happened to glance up into the mounting black. A stick figure stared down at him, circlets of light at its wrists. Their eyes met, the bangles chimed, a new dark surged.

And the sweet-potato vendor of Narrow Alley never looked away again.

After cancer flooded my mother's brain, Ammi brimmed with stories. The tale of the Girl at the Window and the Shakarkandi Vendor of Narrow Alley was one of them.

These stories poured from Ammi's lips with a sick urgency, pieces of her past stitching themselves together until a rich tapestry of her life shone brilliant before my eyes. Stories before Dad and suburbia and Florida and migration. Of a youth spent in Old Lahore near Mosque Wazir Khan in an alley believed to be the narrowest habitable street in Pakistan; where people came and went like thieves slipping through the night.

Why? I guess she wanted them remembered. Wanted the wholesomeness of their truth, their old world strangeness to carry on, no matter how unlikely they seemed.

At first, Dad worried. He wasn't sure how much was too much for a 15-year-old born and bred in good old U.S. of A, but he trusted Ammi and he loved her. Loved her haunted black eyes, her nervous laughter, her café au lait hands, which she painted with henna every Eid.

Ammi was crazy about henna. She knew a woman who knew a desi woman who was a graduate of Rollins College and the finest henna artist in Florida. This lady prepared her own dye by drying, milling and sifting henna leaves, then mixed the dry powder with lemon juice, rainwater, and red wine. To this paste she added eucalyptus and lavender oils to produce rich scented green-brown henna that she packaged in plastic cones. Ammi's adulation of this artist began with an accidental meeting, but soon she was visiting her every few months and they became friends. Ammi loved the smell of her handiwork. She said it reminded her of Lahore's flower gardens and lush lawns in the summer.

When Ammi died, the henna artist came and calligraphed Iqbal's legendary poem 'Love Teaches me the Etiquette of Knowing Myself' on Ammi's torso and her shrivelled arms and hands. The orange and golden hues filled the funeral parlour with my mother's scent. Even after they took her away, the perfume lingered.

It made Dad weepy and volatile for months.

Ammi grew up in Teddy Galli in Old Lahore. You ask Old Lahoris about Teddy Galli and they will laugh. They'll say the architect of this part of inner city hated fat people and designed this 200-feet long alley so it tapers. As you walk down, it narrows until at its tightest it becomes a foot wide and the houses on either side touch foreheads like longing lovers; then Narrow Alley dilates, leads down a gentle slope to a network of criss-crossing streets, and finally opens to the hustle and bustle outside Mochi Gate.

'Where did homeowners park their cars?' I said.

Ammi smiled. She was sitting in the wicker armchair on the lanai, bathed in pink-gold afternoon light. This was her last summer – in two months she would be dead – and she meant to soak in all the heat she could before the underground took her.

'This was the sixties,' she said. A green anole lizard clung to the patio screen a few feet away. The dewlap at its throat pumped, and Ammi watched the blood-red sac bulge against its pebbled skin. 'Nobody in Narrow Alley owned cars. Once these houses were owned by rich merchants and innkeepers, but the Independence War of 1857 against the British left these Muslims and their descendants destitute.'

Although many had bicycles, she added, and these were wheeled through the alley and heaved up and inside the houses.

'Could you get stuck?' I said. 'Anyone ever get stuck in Narrow Alley?' I laughed at the absurdity of the image.

But she was nodding, serious. 'A dirt road two streets down – a farmer lived there. One of his Sahiwali cows escaped from the yard and was chased into the alley by a bunch of children waving sticks. They prodded the panicked animal on until it reached the narrowest part, and there it was wedged. For hours it struggled, lowing and terrified, unable to retreat or move forward. It took the owner and his brothers two hours and twenty feet of rope to drag it out. Flayed in many places by chipped tiles and brickwork, the bleeding creature bellowed until it seemed there was nothing in the alley that night but pain.'

'God, that's awful.'

'Yes,' she said, then added, 'The children were beaten well.'

Originally modelled on Mughal architecture with facades made of faience tiles in ochre and turquoise, the red brick houses of Narrow Alley are at least 200 years old, she said. Small, double story, two fifty-square-foot buildings packed next to each other like cinder blocks. Where the elements destroyed the tile work, successive owners replaced the gaping holes with lime and mortar, rendering these historical homes ugly and listless.

'Why doesn't the government do anything?' I said. 'Don't they care about their culture?'

'Not enough.'

'Can they ask non-profits or UNESCO for help?'

'You can only beg so much,' Ammi said and her voice was strange. The lanai was balmy and claustrophobic and the lizard on the screen swayed back and forth, its beady eyes looking for a way out. Ammi's eyelids flickered, her irises dull against her yellowed sclera.

'Did I ever tell you about the sweet-potato vendor of Narrow Alley?' she said.

I turned my head at this change in subject. 'No.'

'Really?' She didn't seem surprised. 'Not about your Khala Parveen either?'

Ammi's sister died a long time ago was all I knew. She had never talked about Khala in detail. Dad too had made a habit of avoiding mention of her family and life in Pakistan.

'No.'

For a moment she said nothing. Her lips were colourless. 'Zakir, can you please get me my nausea pill?'

I jumped up and ran for the mustard-coloured Zofran. Water spilled from the trembling cup in her hand as she slapped two pills into her mouth and downed them. I watched her nervously. She dropped her head against the chair's back, shut her eyes and began drumming her jagged fingernails on the wooden arms.

After she recovered, she told me the story. I listened and nodded, thinking it was happening already. Her doctor had told us cancer metastases were in peculiar parts of her brain; they could make her cook up surreal histories. 'Confabulation, Mr Assad,' he told Dad. The damn disease would make a liar of my mother.

Was Ammi confabulating? Was she subtracting pain from her childhood and adding uncanny narcotic details best explained by longing and fear? (These two emotions churned together in her.) For a while I believed that and now I hate myself for it. I've come to believe she told me the truth: that there was, in fact, an emaciated girl with a polio-stricken leg who lived in Narrow Alley and her shakarkandi-vending lover who biked up and down her street.

I believe that girl was Ammi's sister, my Khala Parveen.

During one of her frequent breaks to catch her breath, Ammi looked at the sun receding behind the horizon, its crepuscule sharp and poignant. Her eyes were gorgeous. Dusky and gentle, shaped like autumn leaves, they stared at the approaching night. I have never known anyone with eyes prettier than my mother. Not even cancer could touch them.

'How'd your parents feel about that?' I said. 'I mean how'd you guys deal with the affair?' Despite songs of legendary lovers – Heer-Ranjha, Laila-Majnun, Soni-Mahiwal – always on the lips of beggars and flautists in every corner, this was Pakistan in the sixties, and free love, I knew, was forbidden.

'They hated it,' Ammi said, and smiled. 'But they liked it more.'

When Parveen began vanishing at dusk, Ammi was the first to discover it.

Ostracized by the neighbourhood children because of her sister's disability, young and enthralled by the secret, Ammi kept it as a weapon she might wield. *Cripple, cripple!* yelled the boys at both of them when Parveen and Ammi walked to school (one reason Parveen had dropped out of school the year before), and Ammi thought, *Mutant by association, that's what I am.*

She thought this while she watched pale Parveen standing at that window, and she wanted to die.

Ammi imagined she was the only one who knew about the scandal. So Mother's turning to Father one evening as they settled on the charpoy to crack walnuts and peel mangoes dismayed her. A night warm and dangerously still with mosquitoes nipping between their toes, flies buzzing in their ears, and Mother lowered her head towards Father's and whispered, 'Let the girl do what she wants. Don't you say a word. Let her find for herself what we cannot.'

They didn't broach the subject with Parveen. Later, Ammi would try to imagine their parental calculations in order to understand why they wouldn't object to the affair. She made a list of reasons, three of them most pertinent:

Father who inherited the house from a deceased uncle and scraped by with compounding at a rundown dispensary.

Mother who hauled dirty laundry to the dhobi ghaat for others and had forearms thick enough to hold snapping dogs by the neck.

Parveen with her crippled leg that she swung like a bludgeon to see-saw across her bedroom.

Ammi smiled when she described her sister's locomotion, but her eyes were sad. 'I spied on them once or twice. Parveen and her pauper beau. I was fifteen and angry and envious. How could he love her? How could he love my older sister with her humiliating disability and her weird, quiet manner? I couldn't understand it.'

So she stole out and tailed Parveen.

The lovers' ritual rendezvous involved the girl sneaking out of the house, crutches tucked in armpits, then swinging herself down the alley. Across the intersection, down the dirt path with its sad-eyed cattle, past the pond near the gardens, they met under a peepal tree. From its branches, legend said, a Muslim girl hung herself after her clansmen sliced her Sikh lover's throat. Here, the shy vendor boy touched Parveen's diseased leg with his fingers. The girl shivered and Hashim popped chunks of lemon-squeezed shakarkandi into her mouth.

Why do you love me? she whispered to him, eyes clear and frightened. I'm nothing. I mean nothing to anyone.

Be mine, he asked her, fingering her bangles. I'm an orphan who never knew his family. A pretender to health and happiness whose heart is rotten by hurt. Who loves you because your silence is heavier than the crash of a thousand heavenfalls. Who cannot take his eyes off you for to do so would be a blasphemy against your beauty. There's nothing else worth loving, nor will there ever be – so be mine, won't you, jaan? Be the moon that whitens my way.

Here under the haunted tree they made busy negotiating vows of love. Their foreheads joined by ardour's gravity, they murmured blood songs and flesh duets; and Ammi watched from the shadows, enchanted and miserable.

They tell me Ammi died of cancer. I say they're wrong.

It was mourning that aged my mother and killed her. Not her five-year-long unhappy arranged marriage, during which her first husband, a cocaine addict with a temper, beat the crap out of her. Not the brief love affair with another sly, violent man, her flight from Lahore, the migration to America where she met Dad, or the tumour that swelled her left ovary and dribbled into her abdomen until it seeded her gut lining with numerous neoplastic pearls.

My mother didn't die of disease but grief. She perished from longing and wonder.

How could anyone die of *wonder*? you might ask.

To answer that, I'd have to tell you about the rainstorm. I'd have to describe to you the ferocity of the wettest monsoon to ever hit Pakistan. A shrieking, pouring, deluging beast that submerged Lahore in a liquid rage, flooded its impoverished alleys and drowned its Mughal gardens.

But before that, let me tell you how the pale girl, my Khala Parveen, died in that summer of '67.

It was her leg, the traitorous limb that, having once disabled the girl, shook with malignant laughter and betrayed her again.

This time fatally.

A rare bone cancer bloomed from Parveen's femur and surged upward. It sucked the fat from her body and melted the muscle off her limbs so that within weeks she was misshapen and bed-bound. The tumour tunnelled through her lymph nodes and created a fistula that suppurated and oozed blood. She couldn't limp, she couldn't stand, she couldn't even take a shit without bubbles of blood erupting from the opening in her groin. Her eyes sank deeper into her skull, her bangles came loose and fell clattering to the alley. Near the end she couldn't speak because the cancer had pincered the speech centres in her brain.

Through all this Hashim sat by her bedside. His eyes were wide and more feverish than the dying girl's. He had abandoned his shakarkandi basket, deserted his shack with its cracked wooden beams and tin roof, and when Parveen's parents couldn't afford to continue her chemotherapy he sold the bicycle along with his belongings and wagered all the money on her battle with death.

'Night time was the worst,' Ammi said. 'That was when she ached the most. One evening Father went to her room, and Hashim was holding Parveen, stroking her hand. His knuckles gleamed with her sweat. She smelled of rot and incontinence, but his lips didn't leave her skin, not once. Father watched them from the doorway and left without a word. Later, we heard him smash his vials in the workroom and curse loudly, and Mother was afraid to enter.'

Ammi studied the lovers together. Parveen's voice was a grunt now, her words comprehensible only to the vendor boy. Sometimes she had fits and her bitten tongue crept from the corner of her mouth and bled on the piss-stained bed sheets. Occasionally, she became delirious and screamed at Hashim to get his 'filthy, raping' hands off her. This was difficult for the boy to hear who, it seemed, had collected all the love he ever had and in one stroke squandered it on the dying, delirious girl.

How could he still love Parveen? Ammi whispered to herself. How could he bear to be with her, touch her, smell her, change her sheets, clean the inside of her yeasty mouth with a drenched cotton swab, murmur Sufi poetry to her, worship her?

The shakarkandi vendor of Narrow Alley did all these things, propelled by something dark and secret in the twining of their shadows. Parveen had stopped eating and he spooned rice khichri into her mouth and waited for it to stop dribbling before trying again. By then it was late August and the monsoon season was upon them, intermittent bursts of rain slanting into the bedroom. Hashim collected the rainwater in small diyas, chanted Quranic prayers to bless it and coaxed Parveen into sucking at it with a straw.

When the dreaded day came, no one was surprised but him. Parveen's chest had been hitching all morning, the death rattle was loud and insistent in her lungs and by midday she had stopped moving. Her eyes were open, fixed on her emaciated lover who slid off the charpoy, unkempt toes pointing at the alley window, and sat unstaring at the halo of sunlight outside.

'It began to rain and wouldn't stop, and Hashim wouldn't let us bury her,' Ammi said. 'He said she would drown, he cried that she was afraid of water snakes. Mother said the same things all elders say about rainfall and heaven's grief, but fact was it made her room humid and we were all worried about putrefaction – except for Hashim.'

He inserted cotton wicks dipped in incense into her nostrils and washed her body with consecrated rainwater. He wouldn't let Ammi or her parents help. He dressed his love in a spotless shroud, bought a new pair of bangles and slipped them on her wrists. 'You are all I ever see,' he whispered to her as he daubed drops of henna on her palms, chanting the verse from Bulleh Shah again and again. 'Everywhere I turn I see you.' He sat at the head of the charpoy, rubbing kalonji oil into her eyebrows and hair until her scalp shone, and watched the rain stream through the window.

It would be the longest monsoon season in the history of Lahore. The month it rained forever. Old timers murmured uneasy prayers, the radio announced flooding was possible near the Ravi River and the canal system on Upper Mall. The open sewerage ravine near Mochi Gate slowly began to fill up with wet leaves, bird nests, shopping bags, dirty shoes, and Hashim sat by the dead girl, waiting, waiting.

The hakim came to determine the stage of decay and was turned away.

The mullah came to sanctify the body, to urge a quick burial, and was yelled out.

Mother and Ammi tried to convince him to put her in the shed behind the house and Hashim threw himself on her, screaming, 'Please. She's afraid of the dark.'

Mother turned to Father and spoke furiously. He shook his head. She wasn't thinking, he said. He wasn't just humouring the boy; the alley was so narrow that a bier couldn't be carried through it. To take Parveen's body to the graveyard they'd need four able-bodied men to lift the charpoy, take it to the roof, and carry it across the rooftops of 20 houses before they could descend and make the rest of the journey through the alley. In this weather the task would be cumbersome and dangerous, if not impossible.

One hundred excuses to delay the inevitable, and the rain poured. The water table rose, the city sank. The sewerage nullah filled up with dead fish, garbage and branches. The pond near the gardens breached its banks, and the alleys ran with foul, knee-deep water.

'Let me take her home with me,' Hashim begged them. 'I will take her home over my shoulders. My shack is big enough for two. It doesn't mind the dead.'

But that, of course, was foolish, that was grief, and Father, who in his youth was a believer in ancestral honour and once might have killed the vendor boy for such a display, said nothing.

By the end of the week the room smelled awful.

From the relentless barrage, the rainwater stood ankle-high on the stone floor and was beginning to change colour. The odour from Parveen wasn't any better. Ammi refused to go in there, wouldn't even bring Hashim food. Mother turned to Father and said through clenched teeth, 'He's insane. The boy's mad.' Father stood quiet, not meeting Mother's eyes, and still wouldn't say anything to the boy.

Not that Hashim cared. His ribs were serrated shadows under his vest. His collarbones were starvation girdles, the skin over them taut and pale. He looked like a ghost standing vigil over a haunting, and when instead of slackening the storm howled and exploded over Narrow Alley, Hashim covered Parveen's face with the shroud and shut the window.

'Get my daughter out of there,' Mother cried, rainwater

squirming down her face. 'Kick that mad boy out. This is crazy, how can you allow this, how can any father allow this?'

Father gave her a look. 'One who knows his daughter is gone,' he replied and he turned and went into the workroom to collect his valuables.

For he knew, as they all did, that it was a matter of days. Soon the alley and the house would be deluged. If the downpour didn't cease, Old Lahore would swim in floodwater the roads inundated, drowning cattle and bikes. The world inside Mochi Gate would be submerged. They had all heard stories about flash floods in Sind and Baluchistan and in the north. Why not here?

So they carefully packed what they could and began to move out. The dead girl lay in the shadow of her lover, and they removed the copper pots and pans one by one, bundled up the linen, tossed the sheets and dragged the charpoys sideways up the alley to the raised warehouse of a merchant half a kilometre away. (This man made quite a bit of money from renting space to his neighbours during that time.) Others followed suit and Narrow Alley began to empty of life even as it filled with the foetid water rising higher and higher between the houses.

I hate them both, Ammi thought. *Why won't he leave?* She stood at the threshold of Parveen's room. The boy had dozed off and was sniffling in his sleep, his fingers clasping Parveen's leg. His vest was torn in the front and his navel showed, a pale knot that sent Ammi's heart racing. Steeling herself, she splashed through the knee-high water and shook him awake.

'Leave,' she told him.

He stared at her, grime and sleep grain in the corner of his eyes. 'What?'

'Go. I need to bury my sister,' Ammi said. 'Get out of here. She deserves better than this.'

He gripped the edges of Parveen's charpoy and sat up. 'She deserves better than all of us.'

They looked at each other. He scratched the white lines streaking down his cheeks. Outside the window, a siren went off, loud and shrill.

'More floods,' Ammi murmured.

'Perhaps,' he said hopefully, and fell back, fingers twitching on Parveen's body. 'I'll stay with her. You go.'

'Damned if I will,' Ammi said, anger surging through her like a bolt. 'Damned if I'll leave her here to rot with you. You're rotten, you know that. You think you're so saintly, the lover loyal to the end. You're nothing but filth. Nothing but a beggar.'

Hashim's irises were a brown so dark they were black, and they watched Ammi.

'Parveen's pauper beau. Nothing but a seducer. A serpent.' Ammi's vision blurred. She wiped her eyes. 'You killed her. With your false promises. She wasn't beautiful, she was ugly,' and now she was crying, tears hot and blinding like this sweltering monsoon rain that had gouged out the beauty of their lives and filled the hole with dead things.

Her legs wobbled, Ammi swayed, and Hashim got up and came to her and took her in his arms.

'Yes,' he whispered, his breath warm on her hair and comforting. 'It's my fault. Not yours. You go now. I'll take care of her.'

Ammi looked up at him. He had lines and shadows that shouldn't be on a face this young. His hands were big and strong around her shoulders, and the devil overtook her: Ammi reached up and kissed his parched lips, pressing into his mouth.

Hashim's eyes widened. He gripped the side of her head with both hands, then reeled back. They stared at each other across the room, Ammi stunned and filled with wonder at her own daring, Hashim's mouth agape and still moist from the kiss. Something shifted in his eyes, a look Ammi hadn't seen before, and triumph charged through her, albeit briefly.

For at that moment an explosion shook the house and sent them both stumbling.

The sirens were shrieking again. More sizzling bursts of wetness came from the sky followed by the crash of metal on metal, and the world was white noise.

Clapping a hand over each ear, Ammi leapt up. Her gaze was riveted on Hashim who sat swaying on his knees. The vendor boy's forehead was bleeding from a gash.

'Bano,' Father yelled from downstairs. 'Get down here. We need to leave now.'

'Acha, Baba,' Ammi called back and turned to Hashim. 'Are you alright?'

He leaned on the wall and staggered to a stand. 'Yes.'

'What was that? The explosion?'

'A canal head,' he said. 'A bridge.'

She wanted to go to him, but the corner of his lips had tightened. He trudged to the charpoy where Parveen lay and after a moment's hesitation Ammi followed.

'Come with me,' she said. 'Nothing we can do for her.'

He wouldn't look at her. 'No.'

She gripped his arm, it was so thin and lifeless, and tugged at him. To her surprise he didn't resist. His body was limp, his eyes red. He pulled the shroud over Parveen's face, whispering 'I'm sorry. I'm so sorry' and allowed himself to be led away, each step making Ammi more ecstatic. Every muscle in her body hummed, and she dared not contemplate the meaning of this. It was enough that he was following her.

She looked back once before they exited the room and saw that the cloth had slipped off her sister again. Parveen's arm dangled off the bedstead, fingers stirring the standing water. Her eyelids were puffed and open, and dully she watched them leave.

Downstairs by the entrance Father glanced sidelong at Hashim. He said nothing, but Mother exploded: 'Now you walk away, you bastard? Now, you're leaving her.'

'Hush,' said Father, but Mother was already shoving the shakarkandi vendor away, crying.

'Now you let my poor baby drown?' she said.

Hashim's face had lost all color. Ammi held his hand and cried out, 'She's dead. What more can he do?'

'He could've let us bury her,' Mother shrieked. 'My daughter. Oh, my daughter.' She made to go upstairs, but Father caught her arm.

'No,' he said. 'No time now. We need to get our valuables to the warehouse and then I'll return for her.' Not once did he look at Hashim when he said that.

Another explosion came, this one closer, and a fresh torrent of water came raging down the alley and broke against their door. Overhead the sky was a nasty grey, an ugly uniformness that drained Ammi's strength and made her legs unsteady. The bloated carcass of a mule shot by her, and suddenly Ammi wanted out of the house. She wanted to flee.

Without looking at her parents she grabbed Hashim's hand and waded up the alley. He came, limp and shivering from so many days of starving. He was filthier than the slosh eddying around them. They splashed and plowed through waist-high water with several other families abandoning home. Lots of colourful fish struggling upstream, Ammi thought. Later what would these women of Narrow Alley say about her, hanging on to the vendor boy's arm like that? The thought pleased her.

Her parents caught up, quilts and blankets wrapped

in plastic under their arms. Mother cast hateful glances at Hashim who watched the windows lining the alley on either side. Then she and Father overtook them.

Ammi slipped and floundered on, her thoughts circling back to Parveen. Was the water level in her bedroom creeping up? She had already seen flickers in the pool – water snakes? She imagined one slithering up the charpoy, wrapping itself around her sister's ankle. Her bruised greenish skin dimpling as the creature's forked tongue investigated this new territory. Ammi shuddered and tightened her grip on Hashim.

The vendor boy was shaking. His chest hitched.

'What's wrong?' Ammi said.

'I shouldn't have left her.' His face was wet with tears or rain. Malnutrition sores glistened at the corner of his lips. 'She's afraid of the dark.'

'She's dead. Dark is all she has now.'

He stared at her and jerked his arm away. 'What's wrong with you? Who talks about her sister like that?'

She wanted to look defiant, but heat was rushing to her face. She said, 'You don't know what you're talking about. I loved my sister,' and she was startled to discover it was true. She had a mad fondness for Parveen, twisted by her sister's infirmity. She couldn't remember the last time she hadn't felt contempt for Parveen, but mixed with that was admiration and awe at the girl's ability to transcend herself. Wasn't that part of why she had envied her sister Hashim's adoration?

The vendor boy was gazing at the high alley windows, a strange expression on his face. 'Someone's following us,' he said.

'What?' Ammi looked up. Half a dozen windows eyed her on both sides. Some were glazed, others open and empty. 'No one's there.'

'Perhaps.' But his face was doubtful.

Up ahead a door banged open. More men and women, shalwars pulled up to their thighs, scattered out. The floodwater was up to Ammi's breasts now. Strange that it was rising this quickly; it was raining but more drizzle than deluge, and the slope should've kept the level steady. The water was rank. Dead squirrels and rats swept past her followed by shopping bags spinning and juddering, bloated like human heads.

Her gaze went up the alley to its narrowest part where the legendary cow had gotten wedged and flayed. The houses on either side prostrated here so their balconies touched and you could easily jump from one to the other; and at first she thought that was what the figure in the window was trying to accomplish, diving from one house to its opposite, a blur against the pale sky. A narrow human bridge with a bare, trailing leg.

Ammi blinked and it was gone, whatever it was. The strip of sky was unblemished even if it seemed thinner. The gap between the houses was so minute you could reach out and hold hands with your neighbour. Must be the waning daylight, for surely the buildings hadn't nudged closer.

'We better hurry,' Ammi said and her words were drowned by the sudden screech of water geysering from a fire hydrant behind her. The force of the eruption tore her from Hashim's grip and flung her into the ensuing rip tide. She landed face first, the liquid gushing into her lungs, knocking out her breath. Ammi peered into the water, saw something dark and elongated rush past her, tensed her abdomen and kicked hard. As she broke the surface, she saw Hashim standing 10 feet away, looking dazed but unhurt.

Hashim, she tried to yell, but water jetted out of her mouth, burning her throat and chest. Her vision blurred. She coughed and doubled over to let the spasm pass. When she looked up again, the boy was gone.

Ammi lurched. Her legs were trembling, her belly throbbed, and fear coiled at the base of her spine. Her hair was clumped and hung in her eyes. Rain drove at her in cold sheets, small pellets thudding against her flesh, and she thought of a hundred sharp mouths nibbling at her.

She whirled around and saw Hashim hunched in the water 15 feet downstream. His vertebrae were knobby and sharp through his vest like large nails. His arms flailed, as he fought whatever was trying to drag him away. A group of men and women stood near, holding their children on their shoulders. They didn't move to lend him a hand.

'Help,' Ammi yelled. 'Please someone help him.'

'Is he crazy?' someone called back.

'What?'

'There's nothing there. He's just pounding at the water.'

Confused, filled with dread, Ammi thrashed toward him. Her foot landed on something sharp, and she moaned. When she tried to walk, the pain crescendoed till she screamed. Trying to breathe through the throbbing, she hobbled to the nearest door and leaned on it. A trickle of red swirled around her waist and dissipated into the water. A sharp stone or a knife someone dropped? Tottering on one leg, she lifted the injured foot as high as she could and felt the underside. Something was buried in her flesh. She pulled it out and peered at it.

It was a broken shard of yellow glass. A jagged piece once part of a bangle.

Parveen's? Not possible. Their house was at least 200 feet down from here.

She raised her head and her gaze went to the window of the house across the alley. Someone stood in the gloom, slender and pale, hair blackened with water. A girl? Her eyes were milky and shone like cataracts, and they were fixed on Ammi.

Something plopped in the water and Ammi flinched. She had dropped the bangle shard. It sank quickly. She looked up again and saw the window was empty.

'Parveen!' Hashim was screaming ten feet away. 'I'm sorry. I'm sorry, my darling. I won't leave you again.'

Ammi braced herself against the door frame and plunged into the floodwater. She began to paddle towards

Hashim. A lanky man with a labourer's turban had waded closer and was trying to hold his seizing arms. Hashim bucked and flung the man away, then lifted his head. His eyes bulged as they looked at Ammi.

'Wherever I turn I see her drowning,' he shrieked, 'I'm coming, my darling. I'm coming.' And then he dove.

Ammi went after him, but her foot was aching and each kick sent pain razoring through her. She came up for air and saw shadows like black spirals in all the windows of the alley. The girl-shaped darknesses leaned out. Tumour-swollen arms glistened in the dusky light, greenish faces turned to the spot where the struggling vendor boy had been.

Ammi wanted to scream, but when her mouth opened she swallowed floodwater. Her throat was locked. She flopped to a stand and discovered the water lapping at her chin now. She twitched her head up, and the windows gaped at her. No one stood or leaned or beckoned. The vendor boy was gone; he had been underwater for at least two minutes, and the men around him were shaking their heads, already on the move.

Sobbing, Ammi turned and began to swim upstream.

The light was fading fast. The windows were vacant, but all around her came sounds of things falling and splashing in the water, like dozens of human bodies. Whirlpools in front and behind her, which sucked on themselves and faded away. Soft, slimy things brushed her legs, with each touch a fresh panic urging her on faster and faster until, gasping and crying, she reached the narrowest part of the alley, brought her arms together, and shot through.

In 1967 my mother and her parents, along with several neighbours, were flooded out of their homes in Teddy Galli.

Clutching screaming children above their heads, these men and women gasped and lurched sideways through the narrow alley, wading single file in places, front and back against chipped bricks whose edges bit their flesh like piranhas. Careful lest their kids loll into water bubbling past their nostrils, holding their breath against the foetor of sewerage from burst pipes and overflown gutters – the residents of Narrow Alley escaped the worst flooding in Old Lahore's history.

Not everyone was that lucky. Through calamity or governmental negligence many people died that year. The official count of the missing and the dead ran into thousands. One of them was Khala Parveen.

Another was a shakarkandi vendor named Hashim.

'They never found their bodies,' Ammi said.

I massaged her legs. The tips of my fingers left dimples in her flesh. 'Doesn't the Ravi flow close to the city? May be they floated into the river and sank.'

'Perhaps.'

Avoiding the snake-like varices on her skin, I kneaded her flesh. 'You really think you saw a ghost that day?'

Ammi leaned back in the chair.

'But you were dazed by the blow. Half-drowned. It must have been claustrophobic and very, very dark.'

'I don't know what I saw,' she said. The lanai was swollen with shadows. Ammi's cheeks glistened with sweat, she was rolling a Xanax between her fingers. Night time made her nervous. 'I loved my sister,' she added, 'but I also feared her. Sometimes I think that's where my cruelty came from when she was alive. My fear of what she had become.'

'What had she become?'

'A monster.' Her lips trembled. She said, 'That's a lie. She wasn't the monster, we were. She wasn't bitter and angry, I was. When I think of what I did in that room, how I kissed him right in front of her – it was cruel and unfair and wrong. What matter that she was dead? I didn't love him. I just wanted what they had.' She couldn't look at me. 'All my life I've wanted only that.'

I studied my mother in the gloom. There is an Urdu word, which has no English equivalent: *Ishq*. It means the state of a lover's heart during separation, contemplation, or annihilation unto the lover. The point where the lover becomes the beloved. Sometimes it also means nostalgia for a love forever gone, a love that never was, and love that remains after death.

It is not cancer that kills her, I thought as I watched my mother's skeletal mouth form a silent prayer.

That night after she was finished with the story, Ammi walked. She took small and gentle steps, but she didn't look drained—as if bloodletting the past had vitalized her. Dad doesn't believe in garden lamps so the lawn patch behind our house was soft with moonlight. The night was humid, and I had a stuffy nose from a summer cold or allergies. I couldn't breathe comfortably. I watched her pace under the magnolias, southern oaks, junipers, and queen palms, and a misplaced sense of *ishq* settled over me. I've never been to Pakistan, I've never been in love; so what was this pain, this longing to see that alley, that narrowest of streets, where decades ago two people drowned in love or misery?

I was grieving for people I'd never met.

An urge to run to the trees came over me: to throw myself at my mother's feet and cry, *Don't leave me. I know you're dying. You and Dad don't talk about it, you think if you don't talk about it, it will happen painlessly, but it won't. I am hurting every day. I am hurting, Ammi, and I don't know how long the pain will last. Don't leave me, Ammi.*

I watched her meander until she became a shadow amidst shadows. I turned and went into the house. I left her to gaze at the trees, to look for whatever evergreens she might find hidden from last fall.

I went to sleep, letting my mother walk the night forever.

THE WANDERING CITY

On a cool April morning, moments after the muezzin walks, sleep-drunk, to the Mughalpura Mosque and before the discounted holometer at Lahore's Abdus Salam Quantum Centre starts beeping, the City flickers at the edge of a Florida wetland and wanders into Lahore.

Allahrakha is the first to see it. He has just crossed Shalamar Bagh via GT Road on a donkey cart laden with cattle feed when the City appears. One moment there is the hustle of the highway: the milkmen, labourers, city sweeps, and truck drivers wheeling and trilling their way through dawn-emptied streets. The next, the world on Allahrakha's right has vanished. Gone are part of the highway, narrow houses, bakeries, barbecue stalls, Mughal gardens, ill-funded primary schools and grocery shops.

In their place stands the City.

Allahrakha gapes at the gleaming black stone walls, tall like a mountain ridge. As the sun brightens, the walls brighten, until it seems they are burning. It takes Allahrakha a moment before he realizes what he's looking at.

'God protect me, it's true!' he says, his voice filled with awe. 'The wiles of Satan have found us. It's *our* turn.'

Before temptation overtakes him, Allahrakha cracks his whip and trundles atop his donkey cart away to a mundane, safer world.

News of the arrival spreads like a plague. Stall to stall, door to door, alley by alley echoes the whisper: The Enchanted City is here! Yes, *that* City in *our* city!

Wide-eyed Lahoris gather outside the City's rectangular walls as they might at sites of massacre or accidents. Some are friends and family of those on whom the City landed, and these bereaved rend their clothes and wail. Their loved ones are gone and not a trace of them will be found. The eminent cleric, nicknamed Maulana P.J., will be on TV soon to announce a mass funeral in absentia as per the Al-Azhar Consensus; but for now the remaining Lahoris gawk at the City, nudging each other, daring someone to climb the walls.

A foolhardy youth's friends prod him into volunteering. Just a peek, they coax. The tallest truck-mounted telescopic crane they can find is brought and the boy, Subhan, is seated on the boom. The boom is extended to its limit. To no one's surprise – they've all heard the stories – the extended arm's height matches the top of the wall so precisely it looks like it was built to specification.

Everyone cheers.

Subhan steps on to the top of the City wall and gazes down.

An old man shouts up at him, 'Tell us what you see.'

'I see…' Subhan begins, then stops, staring below. The crowd jostles for position and a teen with binoculars trains them on the young man's face. 'You,' Subhan calls, his face bright with wonder. 'How beautiful you are. Oh, were I a speck of dust—'

With that, the young man leaps off the wall and into the City. Moments later there is a thud.

The crowd gasps, shocked by this confirmation. They've watched documentaries about the Enchanted City. Their children follow fanzines and web blogs and YouTube channels. They are in on all the juicy details.

They also know dozens more will volunteer to climb, including some with premeditated plans for a jump.

Just when a man with rat-like features offers to help draw lots for the next 'lucky' climber, there is commotion – screeching tires, a blaring loudspeaker.

The Army has arrived.

The City is barricaded. Barbed wire fences put up. Choppers and drones fly over the walls to discourage trespassers and jumpers. New aerial photos go viral: lofty palaces, golden domes, splendid white terraces rising from unblemished houses, lovely gardens with waterways and fountains, trees bent with ripe fruit and, close to the black walls, a seemingly placid lake on the surface of which prance human figures.

Word is sent to the World Enchanted City Co-operative (WECC) and UNESCO that the ninth-century heritage site has shifted to Lahore. A team of locksmiths is challenged to find any door or hidden mechanism that might provide ground access to the City. Fulfilling expectations, they fail. Civil engineers are called; they arrive debating whether it is a city or a microcity – 'It's two kilometres in length; about a kilometre and a half in width!' exclaims one – and leave with the argument still raging. Heritage architects and artists are invited to examine the City's walls. They find them pristine – not a scratch or gouge. The Enchanted City is meticulous at maintaining itself.

The prime minister and chief of army staff make speeches on TV, declaring a national day of mourning, expressing grief for those lost to the City's relocation and hope that its presence will be good for the economy.

'I want to tell my nation today: *ghabrana nahi hai*,' declares the PM bombastically. 'We must not fear it. We are a country brimming with hidden wonders, unimaginable beauty. The Enchanted City adds to that legacy. Imagine the untapped tourism potential! We will turn this calamity into opportunity.'

Pakistan Tourism Development Corporation's marketing kicks into high gear. Vloggers and bloggers are handsomely paid. Tripadvisor, Condé Nast and other travel sites are contacted to update their databases. Flight traffic to Pakistan increases a hundredfold as EC-chasers, rich louts and bucket-listers swoop in to catch a glimpse of the Enchanted City. Historians, anthropologists, sociologists, biologists, and economists flock to Lahore to study the City and its impact on local populations, human and avian.

Food carts pop up alongside the barricade. Panipuri, papri chaat, mixed chana, coconut water and rosewater sherbet sell out daily before noon. Photo-wallas, cigarette-wallas, toymakers, street magicians, cotton candy men grow rich in weeks. A juice-seller named Bholi makes so much money that he opens a branch on the *other* end of the City near Sheranwala Park.

As per protocol, an MOU is signed between the WECC and the Pakistani government, following which sanctioned visits into the City begin.

'Directly behind us,' says Dr Abida Parveen, Director of the Lahore Museum, as she, a dozen high school students, and seven VIPs disembark from the military chopper that has landed on a greenbelt inside the City, 'now *fussing* at us are the marionettes.'

She points at the gorgeous girls in vibrant robes standing by the stone walls. One thousand and one line the entirety of the City's perimeter. When they see the spectators watching, the girls smile in unison, bat their eyelashes, and gesture to the group to come close. Next to them on blood-darkened ground, which shimmers to look like water, lies Subhan's crushed skeleton, covered in tatters of fabric and skin. The cheels of Lahore and the ravens of the City have finished with him.

'We believe the sirens are the City's sentinel mechanism. Few wall-climbers are able to resist their call.'

'And why do you suppose that is?' asks a dignitary.

'The Magic of the Mutable Marionettes.' The director smiles. 'Or so the old chronicles go. WECC scientists believe the granite at the top of the walls is laced with pheromones and hallucinogens. This was hinted at in animal experiments a few decades ago – before UNESCO and WECC put a stop to such work. There is also an energy signature detected each time a climber locks in on a siren, accompanied by the subtlest shift in the siren's physiognomy. We believe the siren changes features to maximize the potency of its call.'

Dr Parveen leads the VIPs, including siblings of a four-star army general and a cousin of the PM, and the kids through perfectly formed gardens, past carved marble gates and into a market square. The market is crammed with fruit carts, sweetmeats, delicate cutlery and colourful desserts, over which are shoppers bent and haggling and – motionless. Petrified in the act of commerce or argument.

The same vision greets them wherever the dignitaries go: city centre with its twin brass towers, the palaces, verandas, houses and tombs. Parks and gardens filled with animals and humans, sweethearts and sworn enemies, stilled and preserved. One high schooler begins to hyperventilate and is led back to the chopper while the rest hurry to finish their tour of the City before sundown.

'A city haunted by its own people. Forever alive in death,' pronounces the director. 'We believe these to be descendants of Scythian nomadic tribes who converted to Islam and built a city in which to settle – but were trapped in a space-time rift. The trigger remains unknown, although inscriptions discovered by WECC seem to describe "a blight" after the arrival of a mysterious enchantress.'

A student snorts. 'Yeah, blame a woman every time.'

'Magic?' says another. 'You also believe the Redditors who say the City's "a place between the celestial and the terrestrial?"' She makes air quotes.

'The WECC physicists call it *quasiparticle displacement*.'

'Why no midnight tours?' inquires a dignitary. 'What happens at sundown?'

'Why,' says the director, 'the tomb opens.'

When the VIP raises her eyebrow, Dr. Parveen points to an ornate marble tomb as large as a soccer field. It has eight sandalwood doors studded with gemstones and golden nails, surrounded by dozens of sepulchres. 'The tomb opens at dusk and 100 automatons pour out. Anyone remaining in the City is torn to shreds.' She shivers with the thrill of it, and adds thoughtfully, 'Their armour is impregnable.'

'How long does the City stay in one place?' asks a student.

'Three years on average, but anywhere from seven months to five years. Hey, I wouldn't do that!' The director's sharp voice startles the VIP scratching at a ruby on a sandalwood door.

The man backs away, sulking. 'I was just taking a look.'

'Ma'am.' Someone raises a hand. 'Has anyone ever tried to steal the gems?'

The director's smile is cold. 'Yes,' and they follow her gaze to the sepulchres arrayed around the Tomb of Automatons.

For months, Lahoris celebrate and revere the Enchanted City. Flower garlands and ceremonial threads are hung from barricade and barbed wire. During the Basant season, teenagers gather on rooftops and fly kites and drones, with knockoff GoPros and generic cameras, across the City's skyline, taking photos of the tombs, sepulchres, palaces, houses. Pakistani Insta, Twitter and Snapchat fill up with bird's-eye views and selfies and filtered renderings. Nighthawk photos show automatons busily surveilling the

City even as Lahoris drink lassi or bhang and dance around the perimeter all night.

Things come to an unfortunate head when, on a sanctioned trip, the religious scholar Maulana P.J. glimpses the clockwork jinn that trundles out of the City's mosque on a Friday, cups its hands over its mouth and sounds the call to prayer: an eerie, ancient bellow that reaches miles past the walls of the haunted City. Maulana P.J. feels it in his heart, a bass thrum that triggers his atrial fibrillation.

Maulana is carried to the chopper, and instant fatwas are passed against the existence of the Enchanted City. Radio stations blare propaganda against the 'City of Infidels', screaming 'CONSPIRACY: The jinn's an Israeli weapon, the sirens a Hindu plot against our pious boys!' Defend-the-Sharia marchers fill the streets. While most of Lahore watches uneasily from the sidelines, pseudo-mullahs and goons storm the barricades, hooting and spitting at the Army men.

It is feared that riots may break out. An Army hawaldar might be bribed; a sympathetic captain convinced to step aside; the City's walls scaled; the palaces and sepulchres raided; may be a few petrified men killed or women carried off.

Nervously, the prime minister and Army chief watch the anarchy churn. The Enchanted City protects itself. It can be unforgiving: that much is clear from eyewitness accounts dating back to the nineteenth century, when the first sightings were reported. Who knows what might happen if it is truly assailed.

Also, the MOU.

Pakistan will be a pariah, they whisper.

Then, one morning, the City is gone. Lahoris wake up and there is nothing but blankness the size of Old Lahore on GT Road. Army men, food vendors and beggars stand in a circle around the vast emptiness, watching dust blow in veils and shopping bags swirl. They scratch their heads.

'We affronted the inhabitants of the City,' an old beggar offers. 'It might never return.' His eyes mist over. 'And if it does, I might be long dead.'

Slow for a day or two, then so fast it seems a blur, Lahore reclaims the blankness. Appropriately bribed government officials sell the residential plots to a property tycoon for pennies. Lahria Greens will be 'The Community of Your Dreams', the tycoon promises, even as the newspapers report a sudden increase in the number of homeless and jobless jumpers in Lahore. The clever rat-faced man puts up a headstone where Subhan was killed, proclaiming him and the others lost to the City martyrs, and a shrine springs up around it. Pocket Quran-sellers, shoe-shiners, shoe-keepers to watch your chappals when you take them off to pray and rosary makers build a circle of commerce around Subhan. The Lahore Development Authority (LDA) puts up half-hearted warnings against illegal construction, but shopkeepers and traders bring a stay on the proceedings order, so the LDA is forced to watch food stalls wheel in and ugly illegal structures pop up as the court decides on a litigation date.

Months later, a ten-year-old girl who has moved into a Lahria Green home with her family picks up something gleaming in the soil of her backyard and examines it.

It is a brass marionette no bigger than her ring finger. When sunlight hits its eyes, one of them closes so it seems the figure is winking at her, pleased at a shared secret or a promise.

The girl smiles, and, slipping the marionette into her pocket, returns to her games.

RESURRECTION POINTS

I was thirteen when I dissected my first corpse. It was a foetid, soggy teenager Baba dragged home from Clifton Beach and threw in the shed. The ceiling leaked in places, so he told me to drape the dead boy with tarpaulin so the monsoon water wouldn't get at him.

When I went to the shed, DeadBoy had stunk the place up. I pinched my nostrils, gently removed the sea-blackened aluminum crucifix from around his neck, pulled the tarp across his chest. The tarp was a bit short – Ma had cut some for the chicken coop after heavy rainfall killed a hen – and I had to tuck it beneath DeadBoy's chin so it seemed he were sleeping. Then I saw that the fish had eaten most of his lips and part of his nose and my stomach heaved.

After a while I felt better and went inside the house.

'How's he look?' said Baba.

'Fine, I guess,' I said.

Baba looked at me. 'You all right?'

'Yes.' I looked at Ma rolling dough peras in the kitchen for dinner, her face red and sweaty from heat, and I leaned into the smell of mint leaves and chopped onions. 'Half his face is gone, Baba.'

He nodded. 'Yes. Water and flesh don't go well together and the fish get the rest. You see his teeth?'

'No.'

'Go look at his teeth and tell me what you see.'

I went back to the shed and peeled the pale lip-flesh back with my fingers. His front teeth were almost entirely gone, sockets blackened with blood. The snail-like uvula at the back of the throat was half-missing. I peered into his gaping mouth, tried to feel the uvula's edge with my finger. It was smooth and covered with clots, and I knew what had happened to this boy.

'So?' Baba said when I got back.

'Someone tortured him,' I said. Behind Baba, Mama sucked breath in and fanned the manure oven urgently, billowing smoke away from us toward the open door.

'How do you know?' Baba said.

'They slashed his uvula with a razor while he was alive, and when he tried to bite down they knocked out his teeth with a hammer.'

Baba nodded. 'How can you tell?'

'Clean cut. It was sliced with a blade. And there are no teeth chips at the back of the throat or stuck to the palate to indicate bullet trauma.'

'That wouldn't be the only sign of bullet entry. Not bad, though.' Baba looked pleased. He tapped his chin with a spoon and glanced at Mama. 'You think he's ready?'

Mama tried to lift the steaming pot, hissed, let it go and grabbed a rough cotton rag to hold the edges. 'Now?'

'I was his age when I did my first.' He looked at me. 'You're old enough. Eat your dinner. Later tonight I'll show you how to work them.'

We sat on the floor and Ma brought lentil soup, vegetable curry, raw onion rings and cornflour roti. We ate in silence on the meal mat. When we were done we thanked Allah for his blessings. Ma began to clear the dinner remains, her bony elbows jutting out as she scraped crumbs and wiped the mat. She looked unhappy and didn't look up when Baba and I went out to work the DeadBoy.

DeadBoy's armpits reeked. I asked Baba if I could stuff my nostrils with scented cotton. He said no.

We put on plastic gloves made from shopping bags. Baba laid the boy on the tools table, situating his palms upward in the traditional anatomical position. I turned on the shed's naked bulb and it swung from its chain above the cadaver, like a hanged animal.

'Now,' Baba said, handing me the scalpel, 'locate the following structures.' He named superficial landmarks:

jugular notch, sternal body, xiphoid process, others familiar to me from my study of his work and his textbooks. Once I had located them, he handed me the scalpel and said: 'Cut.'

I made a midline horizontal and two parallel incisions in DeadBoy's chest. Baba watched me, shaking his head, frowning, as I fumbled my way through the dissection. 'No. More laterally' and 'Yes, that's the one. Now reflect the skin back, peel it slowly. Remove the superficial fascia' and 'Repeat on the other side'.

DeadBoy's skin was wet and slippery from water damage and much of the fat was putrefied. His pectoral and abdominal musculature was dark and soft. I scraped the congealed blood away, removed the fascia, and as I worked muscles and tendons slowly emerged and glistened in the yellow light, displaying neurovascular bundles weaving between their edges. It took me three hours but finally I was done. I stood, surrounded by DeadBoy's odour, trembling and peering at my handiwork.

Baba nodded. 'Not bad. Now show me where the resurrection points are.' When I hesitated, he raised his eyebrows. 'Don't be nervous. You know what to do.'

I took a glove off and placed it on DeadBoy's thigh. I tentatively touched the right pec major, groping around its edges. The sternal head was firm and spongy. When I felt a small cord in the medial corner with my fingers, I tapped it lightly.

The pec didn't twitch.

I looked at Baba. He smiled but his eyes were black and

serious. I licked my lips, took the nerve cord between my fingers, closed my eyes and discharged.

The jolt thrummed up my fingers into my shoulder. Instantly the pec contracted and DeadBoy's right arm jerked. I shot the biocurrent again, feeling the recoil tear through my flesh, and this time DeadBoy's arm jumped and flopped on to his chest.

'Quite something, isn't it,' Baba said. 'Well done.'

I didn't reply. My heart raced, my skin was feverish and crawling. My nostrils were filled with the smell of electricity.

'First time's hard, no denying it. But it's gotta be done. Only way you'll learn to control it.'

I was on fire. We had talked about it before, but this wasn't anything like I had expected. When Baba did it, he could smile and make conversation as the deadboys spasmed and danced on his fingertips. Their flesh turned into calligraphy in his hands.

'That felt like something exploded inside me, Baba,' I said, hearing the tremble in my voice. 'What happens if I can't control it?'

He shrugged. 'You will. It just takes time and practice, that's all. Our elders have done it for generations.' He leaned forward, lifted DeadBoy's hand, and returned it to its supine position. 'Want to try the smaller muscles? They need finer control and the nerves are thinner. Would be wise to use your fingertips.'

And thus we practiced my first danse macabre. Sought out the nerve bundles, made them pop and sizzle, watched the cadaver spider its way across the table. With each discharge, the pain lessened, but soon my fingers began to go numb and Baba made me halt. Carefully he draped DeadBoy.

'Baba, are there others?' I asked as we walked back to the house.

'Like us?' He nodded. 'The Prophet Isa is said to have returned men to life. When Martha of Bethany asked him how he would bring her brother Lazarus back to life, Hazrat Isa said, "I am the resurrection and the life. He who believes in me will live, even though he dies."'

We were in the backyard; the light of our home shone out bright and comforting. Baba turned and smiled at me. 'But Hazrat Isa was a healer first. Like our beloved Prophet Muhammad Peace-Be-Upon-Him. Do you understand?'

'I guess,' I said. DeadBoy's face swam in front of my eyes. 'Baba, who do you think killed him?'

His smile disappeared. 'Animals.' He didn't look at me when he tilted his jaw and said, 'How's your friend Sadiq these days? I haven't seen him in a while.'

'Fine,' I said. 'He's just been busy, I think.'

Baba rubbed his cheek with a hairy knuckle and we began walking again. 'Decent start,' he said. 'Tomorrow will be harder, though.' I looked at him; he spread his arms and smiled, and I realized what he meant.

'So soon?' I said, horrified. 'But I need more practice.'

'Sure, you do, but it's not that different. You did well back there.'

'But—'

'You will do fine, Daoud,' he said gently and would say no more.

Ma watched us approach the front door, her face silvered by moonlight. Baba didn't meet her eyes as we entered, but his hand rose and rubbed against his khaddar shirt, as if wiping dirt away.

Later huddled on the charpoy, staring through the skylight at the expansive darkness, I heard them arguing. At one point, I thought Ma said, 'Worry about the damn house.' He tried to shush her, but she said something hot and angry and Baba got up and left. There was silence, then there was sobbing. I lay there, filled with sorrow and excitement, listening to her grief, thinking if only there was a way to reconcile the two.

The dead foot leaped when I touched the resurrection point. Mr Kurmully yelped.

'Sorry,' I said, jerking my fingers away. 'Did that hurt?'

'No.' He massaged the foot with his hand. 'I was… surprised. I haven't had any feeling in this for years. Just a dry burning around the shin. But when you touched it there' – he gestured at the inner part of his left ankle – 'I *felt* it. I felt you touching me.'

He looked at me with awe, then at Baba, who stood by the door, hands laced behind his back, looking pleased. 'He's good,' Mr Kurmully said.

'Yes,' Baba said.

'So when are you retiring, Jamshed?'

Baba laughed. 'Not for a while, I hope. Anyway, let's get on with it. Daoud,' he said to me, 'can you find the pain point in his ankle?'

I spent the next 30 minutes probing and prodding Mr Kurmully's diabetic foot, feeling between his tendons for nerves. It wasn't easy. Over the years, Mr Kurmully had lost two toes and the stumps had shriveled, distorting the anatomy. Eventually I found two points, braced myself, and gently shot them.

'Feel better?' I said, as Mr Kurmully withdrew his foot and stepped on it tentatively.

'He won't know until tomorrow,' Baba said. 'Sometimes instant effect may occur, but our true goal is nocturnal relief when the neuropathy is worst. Am I right, Habib?'

'Yes.' Mr Kurmully nodded and flexed his foot this way and that. 'The boy's gifted. I had some burning when I came. It's gone now. His first time?'

'Yes.'

'Good God.' Mr Kurmully shook his head. 'He will go far.' He came toward me and patted me on the head. 'Your father's been a boon to our community for 20 years, boy. Always be gentle like him, you hear me? Be humble. It's the branch laden with fruit that bends the most.' He smiled at me and turned to Baba. 'Let me pay you this once, Jamshed.'

Baba waved a hand. 'Just tip the Edhi driver when he takes the cadaver. One of their volunteers has agreed to bury it for free.'

'They are good to you, aren't they.'

Baba beamed. He opened his mouth to speak, but there was a sudden commotion at the front of the clinic and a tall, gangly man with a squirrel tail mustache strode in, followed by the sulky-faced Edhi driver looking angry and unhappy.

Baba's gaze went from one to another and settled on the gangly stranger. 'Salam, brother,' Baba said. 'How can I help you?'

The gangly man pulled out a sheaf of papers. He had gleaming rat eyes that narrowed like cracks in cement when he spoke. He sounded as if he had a cold. 'Doctor sahib, you know why I'm here.'

'Why don't you tell me, anyway? Would you like to take a seat?'

'Just read the papers, sahib,' he said in his soft, nasal voice and held them out.

'Oh?' Baba looked at the Edhi driver. He was a gloomy, chubby boy fond of charas, and often rolled joints, one hand on his fat belly, when waiting at red lights. I had ridden with him a couple of times and once he showed me his weird jutting navel. Everted since birth, he told me proudly.

'Zamir, what's going on?' Baba said.

'Sahib, they're giving us trouble with the burial,' Zamir

said. 'This man is from the local Defend-the-Sharia office. They have a written fatwa stating that since the dead boy was Christian he cannot be buried in a Muslim cemetery.'

Baba turned back to the gangly man. 'Is that true, brother?'

Gangly Man thrust the papers into Baba's hands. 'This is from Imam Barani. Take a look.'

Baba held the papers by their edges. 'This boy,' Baba said, 'was tortured by someone.'

Gangly Man's shoulders stiffened.

'He was badly beaten. His teeth knocked out with a hammer. Someone took a razor to his mouth. When he was near dead, they threw him in the river.'

Gangly Man's lips pressed into a thin, white line.

'He was 16. He had a scar on his stomach from a childhood surgery, probably appendectomy. He wore a tawiz on his forearm, which his mother likely got from a Muslim saint. You know how illiterate these poor Christians are. Can't tell the difference between one holy man and another, and—'

'Doctor sahib.' Gangly Man leaned forward and said conspiratorially, 'He and his filthy religion can ride my dick. My orders are simple. He will not be buried in the Muslim cemetery, and if I were you I wouldn't push it.' He grinned and shook his head as if talking to a child.

Baba's face changed colour. He looked around and for the first time I saw how angry and tired he was. He looked like he hadn't slept in days. May be he hadn't. It was hard to know. He and Ma were talking less to each other lately.

'If you make it difficult for us, well, things could go many ways, couldn't they? Sometimes clinics run by quacks can be shut down by the government until regulatory inspections are completed. I don't even see a diploma on your wall. Surely, you went to medical school?' Still smiling, he toed the foot of the threadbare couch, the only piece of furniture in the room. 'Besides, you might be Muslim but blasphemy is blasphemy, brother, and punishable under the Hadood Ordinance. The boy is Christian. That cemetery is not.'

The Edhi driver took Baba's arm and led him aside. They talked. Zamir gestured furiously. Baba's shoulders rose and sagged. They came back.

'We will take the body to Aga Khan Medical College and donate it to their anatomy lab,' cried Zamir.

'But he has already been—' Baba began.

'I'm sure they will find more to do with it,' Zamir said, nodding and smiling.

Gangly Man took the front of his own shirt with a tarantula-like hand and began to fan his chest with it. 'Very wise. How they will appreciate you!'

Baba remained silent, but a heavy ice block appeared in my belly and settled there. I turned and ran from the clinic all the way to our house three streets down. I burst into the shed and went to DeadBoy and wrenched away the tarp. His insides were tucked in with thin stitches. I yanked the stitches out, peeled back his skin, and pressed my gloveless fingers into his muscles. I discharged the biocurrent again and again until his limbs twirled and snapped, a lifeless dervish whirling around his own axis. I let the electricity flow through my fingertips like a raging torrent, until the room sizzled with charge and my nostrils filled with the odour of burnt flesh.

After a while I stepped back. My cheeks burned and the corners of my eyes tickled. Even though it was close to noon, the shed was dark from a low-hanging monsoon ceiling. Interstices of sunlight fell on DeadBoy's half-face, revealing the blackness of his absent teeth and his mutilated lips.

'Sorry, DeadBoy,' I said.

He twitched his shoulder.

The movement was so unexpected that I jerked and fell over the toolbox on the floor. I sat on the ground, gazing at DeadBoy, my heart pounding in my chest. He was still. Had I imagined it? That movement – it was impossible. The deadboys couldn't move without stimulus.

I got up and went to him. His disfigured flesh was placid and motionless.

'Hey,' I whispered, feeling foolish and nervous. 'Can you hear me?'

The shadows in the room deepened. Somewhere outside a swallow cheeped.

DeadBoy never said a word.

After the Edhi driver hauled DeadBoy away, I walked around for a while. Soon it began to drizzle, the kind of sprinkle that makes you feel hot and damp but never really cool, so I took off my shirt, tucked it into my armpit, and ran bare-chested to Sadiq's house.

He lived in the Christian mohalla near Kala Pul, a couple of kilometres away. His two-room tin-and-timber house was next to a dirty canal swollen with rainwater, and the smell of rot filled the street.

His mother opened the door. Khala Apee was a young-old woman. Her cheeks were often bruised. Her right eye was swollen shut today.

'He's at the Master sahib's,' she told me in a hoarse voice. She smoked cigarettes when her husband was not home, Sadiq had told me. 'He'll be back in an hour. Want a soda?'

They couldn't afford sodas. It was probably leftover sherbet from last Ramadan. But what was Sadiq doing at Master sahib's? Summer vacation wouldn't be over for another month. 'Thank you, but no, Khala Apee. I'll wait outside.'

She nodded and tried to smile. 'Let me know if you want something. And if you can, do stay for dinner.'

Plain roti with sliced onions. No gravy. 'I'll try, Khala Apee. May I borrow a plastic bag?'

She brought me one. I went to the charpoy under the elm where we sat and made fun of our families. Rain pattered on the elm leaves and hissed on the ground, and as I sat there with my plastic-draped head on the steeple of my fingers I thought about Baba and Ma and how they had been arguing for months. Ma was worried about the house; she wanted Baba to start charging patients. Baba refused. His father and grandfather had never charged a fee, he said. They lived on food and gifts people gave them.

Ma laughed bitterly. Those were different times, you fool. So different. And the house, what about the house, Jamshed? We are in debt. So much debt. What will you do when they come to take our home? If you cared as much about your family as you do about your goddamn corpse learning, we could live like normal people.

But we're not normal, Baba protested. This is a good way to blend in, to be part of this world. Be part of the community—

Blend in? Mama said. We will never blend in if you keep antagonizing them. What was the point of arguing with that mullah? You know they are dangerous people. You keep going like this, we will never be part of the community. How could we be? We are—

Sadiq was shaking me awake. 'Hey, Daoud, hey. Wake up.'

I opened my eyes. 'Hey, how was…*what*?' I said when I saw his face. Sadiq was a small boy with mousy features, and at the moment his features were chiselled with worry.

'You've got to leave, Daoud,' said Sadiq, glancing around. 'Now.'

'What's going on? Everything okay?'

'Yes. Master sahib had heard some rumours and he

wanted to warn us. He—' Sadiq gnawed at his lip, his fingers still tugging at my arm. 'Go home. We'll talk tomorrow.'

'Why?' But he was already leading me away from the elm and toward the canal. The drizzle had stopped and the canal water eddied gently. I put on my shirt and watched as Sadiq took a tin box from his pocket and tied a brick around it with jute twine and twice-doubled rubber band. He waded into the shallow canal and deposited the box at a spot two feet from the bank.

'What are you doing?' I said when he climbed back up the embankment.

'Nothing,' he said, but his voice was strange. 'Run back home now. I'll come by in a couple days if I can.'

I went up the canal road, occasionally looking back, trying to make sense of what had just happened. Sadiq stood there, hands in the pockets of his shorts, a skinny, brown boy with a sad face and a fake-silver cross gleaming around his neck. Sometimes even now I see that cross in my dreams, throwing silver shadows across my path as I trudge down alleys filled with heartache and bodies.

As I glanced back one last time, Sadiq took off the cross and slipped it into his pocket.

Baba was waiting for me.

'Where were you?' he said, his eyes hard and red. 'I was worried sick.'

'At Sadiq's. I wanted to—'

'Foolish boy,' he said. 'Don't you know how dangerous that was? Don't you realize?' I stared at him. He saw my incomprehension and his voice softened. 'Someone vandalized a church in Lahore yesterday. Someone else found faeces strewn in a mosque in Quetta. As a result, two people are dead and tens more injured in riots around the country. These tensions have been building for a while. You saw what that Defend-the-Sharia asshole did this morning. This will only get worse. You cannot visit Sadiq until things settle down.'

'But what does Sadiq have to do with that?'

Baba gazed at me with pity. 'Everything.'

I met his eyes and whatever was in them frightened me so much that my hands began to shake. Quickly I walked past him and went to my room, where I sat on my rickety charpoy and watched dusk seep in through the skylight. In the other room, Ma prayed loudly on the musallah. She might have been crying, I couldn't tell. I tried to read a medical textbook Baba gave me for my last birthday, but my mind was too restless, so I gave up and went to the kitchen where Ma had arranged raw chicken breasts on a chopping board.

I laid my hands on the meat. I thought about Sadiq and his tin box and let the current flow. The chicken breast jumped and thudded on the wood. I discharged again, this time with more force, removed my hands, stepped back, and watched as for a whole minute the meat slapped up and down, squirting blood that puddled on the wooden board, making curious dark shapes.

That should have been impossible but clearly wasn't.

In school during physics class our teacher had explained capacitors to us. Strange ideas came to me now. Words that Baba taught me from his textbooks: cell membranes, calcium-gates, egg-shaped mitochondria and polarized ionic channels. Could *they* act as capacitors at times and hold charge so the flesh would stay alive even after I removed my fingertips?

The boy is gifted, someone said in my head.

I should have felt better. Instead I felt angry and miserable. I went to Ma's room and opened the door.

She was sitting on her haunches in front of the only pretty piece of furniture in the room, a mahogany dresser Baba's mother gave her as a wedding present. Ma had been fiddling with a half-open drawer, a jewellery box glittering in her hand. When I entered, she plunged the drawer into place. 'Are you so disrespectful now that you won't knock?'

'Sorry, Ma. I wasn't thinking.'

'Idiot boy,' she said quietly. Her gaze drifted down to the box she held, her fingers sliding up and down its metallic edges. The space beneath her eyes was dark and wet. 'Next time, mind your manners.'

I thought it prudent to keep my mouth shut. Ma lifted the lid and gazed within and her eyes turned inward. The effect was so intense that for a moment she looked dead. Uneasy, I took a step forward and peered inside. A picture of a naked man nailed to a cross, surrounded by wailing people; then Ma was snapping the lid back into place so violently that I jerked and fell back.

Ma's hands shook and she said something that didn't make sense, 'Never wanted to come here. Your father made me. I never wanted to leave my people,' and she glared at me hatefully. It was a brief moment, but few things in my life since have made me feel so ashamed. So lonely and self-loathing – a mutant child broken and hated.

I turned and ran from the room, blinded by anger or tears, while my mother watched me from the darkness of her room, the jewellery box in her callused hands.

Later they told us it was an accident, that a shanty caught fire and set the mohalla ablaze, but we all knew better.

It was the tail end of monsoon season and the rains had petered out, which worsened the inferno. Fifty Christian houses burned that night; the flames and smoke ceiling could be seen from as far as Gulshan Iqbal, we were told. Twenty people died; Sadiq's father, (who survived tuberculosis and, later, the '99 Kargil War) was among them. Their corpses were pulled out from the wreckage, burnt and malformed. Sadiq's mother recognized her husband only by the hare-shaped mole on his foot.

When I went to see Sadiq, he sobbed on my shoulder.

'They took everything,' he said. 'Our house, our possessions. My father. They burnt the house down. My cousin saw them, I swear to God.'

My right arm was around him. My left hand dug so hard into my thigh I popped the blood blister a biocurrent discharge had raised on my finger. '*Which* God?'

He stared at me with bloodshot eyes, while his mother sat stone-like on the charpoy under the elm, rocking back and forth. One hand tapped the bruises on her cheek. The other hid her lips.

I held Sadiq for as long as I could, then I went home, where Ma sat knitting a cotton sweater. Winter would come in three months, and we couldn't afford to buy new clothes. Baba was out – he'd been delayed at the clinic – so I sat at Ma's feet and counted her toes. Ten.

She watched me through the emptiness between her needles and said, 'I'm sorry.'

'Yes.'

'It was horrible, wasn't it?'

'Yes.'

'Why don't we take Sadiq and his mother some naan and beef korma tomorrow? I'm sure his mother is too upset to cook right now.'

I recalled Khala Apee's vacuous stare, the hand covering her mouth, and nodded.

Ma put her knitting needles down, lowered herself to the floor, and hugged me.

'The world is a bad place,' she whispered. 'We're in

danger all the time. People who are different like you, like us…can sometimes seem like a threat to others.'

I listened. Outside, thunder cracked. The skylight rippled with water as the night opened.

'You use your gift to heal others, you hear me?' she said. 'Don't get consumed by anger or hatred or sides. There are no sides. Only love and not-love.'

Behind me the door banged open. My left eye twitched, the vision in it dimmed transiently, and cleared. Ma sprang to her feet.

'Zamir?' she said. 'What is it?'

'Your husband,' Zamir said. The Edhi driver's hair was dark from rain. His cotton shirt was soaked and his weird navel protruded through it like a hernia.

'What about him?' Ma's voice was full of fear. 'What happened?'

Zamir had a look on his face I had never seen before. 'There was an incident at the clinic.'

Ma stared at him, eyes wide, then comprehension dawned in them and she screamed. It was a sudden noise, sharp and unfamiliar, and it wrenched the air out of me. I shrank back and clutched the end of Ma's love couch, and the knitting needles slipped and fell to the floor, forming a steel cross.

'No,' Ma said. Her hair was in her eyes. She clawed it away, looked at Zamir, and howled again. 'Please don't let it be true. I told him to be careful. I *told* him.'

Zamir's face was ashen.

I scrabbled blindly on the floor. The steel cross glinted at me. Pinching the skin of my thighs, I hauled myself up, feeling the world flicker and recede. Zamir was holding Ma's hand and speaking gently. Your husband went to the police, he was saying. He reported the Christian boy's mutilated body. Some people didn't like that. Then someone discovered an old marriage certificate with *your* maiden name on it.

Ma yanked her hand away from Zamir's. 'I killed him,' she whispered. Her fists flew to her chest and beat it once, then again and again. She rushed to the door, she shrieked at the rain, but the night was moonless.

Bewildered and crying, I thought about the tin box Sadiq hid in the canal when he realized they would be attacked. I thought about dead bodies and festering secrets; of limbs thrashing on a healer's fingertips; of the young Christian boy who was tortured to death. I thought of how 'Daoud' could have been 'David' in a different world, such a strange idea, that. Most of all I thought about the way the chicken breast thrummed under the influence of my will, how it kept jerking long after I took my hands away. Would Baba whirl if I touched him, would he dance a final dance for me?

I wiped my tears. From the crevasse of the night rain the colour of old blood blood gushed and pawed at my eyes. Then we went in Zamir's rickshaw to bring home my father's corpse.

Someone once told me dust has no religion.

Perhaps it was the maulvi sahib who taught me my first Arabic words – a balding kind, quiet man with a voice made for chanting godly secrets and a white beard that flowed like a river of Allah's nur. Five feet away the gravedigger shovelling and turning the soil now looked a bit like him. His string vest was drenched with sweat, even though the ground was soft and muddy from the downpour.

Perhaps it was Ma. Standing next to me before this widening hole, she leaned on Khala Apee, as if she were an axed tree about to fall. Her lips moved silently all the time. Whether she prayed or talked to Baba's ghost, I don't know.

Or perhaps it was Baba who lay draped in white on the charpoy bier under the peepal tree. The best cotton shroud we could afford rippled in the graveyard wind. It was still wet from his last bath. Before they log rolled him on to his back, the men of our neighbourhood had asked me if I wanted to help wash him. I said no. My eyes never brimmed.

Now I let a fistful of forgiving dust run through my fingers. It whispered as it fell, a gentle earthskin shedding off me and on to Baba's face. It would carry the scent of my flesh, let him inhale my presence. I bent and, with a finger, brushed my father's lips, so white, so cold, and a ghastly image came to me: Baba juddering on my fingertips as I reach inside his mouth, shock his tongue and watch it thrash like a bloodied carp. Tell me who murdered you, I tell my father's tongue. Talk to me, speak to me. For I am the resurrection and whosoever believes in me will live again.

But his tongue didn't quiver. It was speechless.

Ma touched my shoulder and drew me back. Her mouth was a pale scar in her face. She gripped my fingers. I looked down, saw that she had coloured her hand with henna and dropped it.

A shiny flaming orange heart, lanced in the middle, glistened on her palm.

It was dark enough to feel invisible. I left Ma praying in her room and went to Kala Pul.

Lights flickered in the streets and on chowrangis. Sad-faced vendors sold fake perfumes and plastic toys at traffic signals. Women with hollow eyes offered motia bracelets and necklaces, and the flower's scent filled my nose, removing Baba's smell in death. Children fished for paan leaves and cigarette stubs in puddles, and I walked past them all.

Something dark lay on the road under a bright fluorescent median light. An alley cat, a starved, mangy creature with a crushed back. Tread marks were imprinted on its fur; clots glistened in them. A chipped fang hung from one whisker.

I didn't know my hand was on it until I saw my fingertips curve. They pressed into the carcass like metal probes seeking, seeking. I didn't even need to feel for a point. In death, the creature's entire body was an enormous potential ready to be evoked.

I met the cat's lifeless eyes reflecting the change of traffic light from green to red. I discharged.

A smell like charred meat, like rust on old bicycle wheels. The creature arched its spine, its four legs locking together; so much tension in its muscles, they thrummed like electric wires. Creaking, making a frothing sound, the alley cat flopped over to its paws and tried to stand.

It lives, I thought and felt no joy or satisfaction.

Blood trickled from the creature's right eye. It tried to blink but the left eye wouldn't open. It was glued shut with postmortem secretions.

My hand was hurting. I shook it, brought it before my eyes. A large bulla had formed in the middle of the palm, blue-red and warm. Gently rubbing it, I got up and left, leaving the newly risen feline tottering around the traffic median, strange sounds emitting from its throat as if it were trying to remember how to mewl.

Deep inside the Christian mohalla I waded through rubble, piles of blackened bricks and charred wood. I stood atop the destruction and imagined the fire consuming rows upon rows of these tiny shacks. Teetering chairs, plywood tables, meal mats, dung stoves, patchworked clothes – all set ablaze. Bricks fell, embers popped, and shadow fingers danced in the flames.

I shivered and turned to leave. Moonlight dappled the debris, shadows twisted, and as I made my way through the wreckage I nearly tripped over something poking from under a tin sheet.

I stooped. The object was a callused human hand, knuckles bruised and hairy like my father's. Blood had clotted at the wrist and formed a puddle below the sharp edge of the tin.

A darkness turned inside my chest; rivers of blood pounded in the veins of my neck and forehead. I don't know how long I sat in the gloom, in that sacred silence. Head bowed, fingers curled around the crushed man's, I crouched, my eyes closed, and groped for the meat of the city with my other hand. I felt for its faint pulse, I looked for its resurrection point; and when the dirt moved and a sound like ocean surf surged into my ears, I thought I had found it.

I stiffened my shoulders, touched the dead man's palm, and let the current flow. The hand jerked, the fingers splayed. A sigh went through the shanty town. Somewhere in the dark, bricks shifted. The ruins were stirring.

Something plopped on the tin sheet. I looked down. Fat drops of blood bulged between my clenched knuckles. I let the dead hand go (it skittered to a side and began to thrash). I opened my fists and examined them.

A crop of raised, engorged bullas on my palms. One amidst the right cluster had popped and was bleeding. The pain was a steady ache, almost pleasant in its tingling. As I watched, blisters on the left palm burst as well and began to gush. Dark red pulsed and quivered its way down my wrists.

Trembling, I crouched on my haunches and grasped the dead man's convulsing limb with both hands. I closed my eyes and jolted the Christian mohalla back to life. Then I sat back, rocking on my heels, and waited.

They came. Dragging their limbs off sparkling morgue tables, slicing through mounds of blessed dirt, wrenching free of rain-soaked grass, my derelict innocents seized and twitched their way across the city. I rose to my feet when they arrived, trailing a sewerage nullah odour behind them that drowned the memory of the motia. Metal rattled and clanged as my last finally managed to crawl out from under the tin sheet and joined the ranks of the faithful.

I looked at them, my people, faces shining with blood and fervour. Their shredded limbs dangled. Autopsy incisions criss-crossed their flesh. Blackened men, women and children swaying in rows, waiting for me. How unafraid, joyous, and visible they were.

I raised my chin high and led my living thus on their final pilgrimage through this land of the dead.

THE FORTUNE OF SPARROWS

The courtyard of the orphanage was haunted by birds.

Songbirds, sparrows, gray hornbills, yellow-footed green pigeons, starlings, crows – every species ever glimpsed in Lahore. Twice or thrice a week they came in doles and murders and murmurations, swooping down and carpeting the roof and the walls.

To this day I've not figured out where they came from in such large numbers or why they gravitated to the orphanage at peculiar intervals. Unsatisfactory theories involving magnetism and satisfactory gossip about corpses buried under the old housing were flung about, but no one could explain why on arrival these birds were so quiet: they would neither cheep nor caw, nor a warbler warble. Hushed, they clung to the courtyard trees, congregated on high wires running parallel to the enclosure walls from one electric pylon to another. It was a sight that gave many a twilight visitor pause when they first glimpsed these silent sentinels. At least until the muezzin called the maghrib prayer and, suddenly, the courtyard came alive with the sound of bird music, the notes of the melodies in harmony with bird colours. The warbler, the cuckoo, the bulbul, the mynah – how they would sing!

For a long time now I have been afraid of birds.

But, back then, living in the orphanage with my sisters, playing baraf pani when it drizzled, listening to the gurgle of water sluicing off rain gutters into the courtyard's red earth, I was not. I liked them. All us girls did. We picked their feathers off the ground and made garlands out of them. We looked for bird nests in the courtyard trees and giggled when Mano stalked them, his mangled tail bristling, and, from hidden corners, sprang at the crows, parrots, and pigeons, making the creatures explode skyward in a flurry of black, blue and green. The colour specks circled the enclosure until night crept up from the horizon and took the birds with it.

Mano the wedding cat belonged to Bibi Soraiya, who managed the orphanage's affairs. Mano was old and two-coloured. Neha used to say that was why prescience boiled in his blood – that he was a creature fleshed from opposites and could glimpse things we could not. Angels, jinns and the ghosts of martyrs walk among us, and everyone knows spirits are fond of cats. Who knew what they whispered in his ear when they floated past him or brushed his fur?

And when Mano settled down by the orphanage gate,

licking his fur and purring, we knew the Rishtay Wali Aunty was to come for us that day or night.

The wedding cat was never wrong about the matchmaker's arrival.

My sisters and I were fond of Mano – we fed him from our plate – but sometimes, when the wedding cat's eyes gleamed in the darkness and he slid across the courtyard, back arched, the sounds from his throat indistinguishable from the rumble of a motor engine outside the orphanage door or the passage of something large and ponderous high above the clouds, we weren't so fond of him.

Sometimes we wished Mano would run away and not come back.

The orphanage was a house of many doors.

A long time ago, during the British Raj, we were told, it was a hospital with two wings that flanked the courtyard. The east wing was the smaller building with limited rooms for dying or contagious patients, as if they were the same. It had a long corridor that ran parallel to the courtyard and formed a semicircle connecting it with the west wing, where the rest of the patients were housed.

These rooms were ours now and we loved playing in them. There were mirrors above the washbasin, and we pretended that people from the past still stayed within our rooms, that the change of the morning and afternoon light in the mirrors meant they were stirring and moving about and such cohabitation made us all a big family. The lives of our family spanned centuries.

I remember one afternoon when we were playing baraf pani. Barefoot, we rushed at the fleeing team, trying to touch theirs arms or torsos, to pretend-petrify them into captivity. The escapees would circle back and try to tap the captives 'awake'. Half of my sisters were already statues frozen by the chasing team, but Neha cheated by hiding, which wasn't allowed.

It had rained the night before. The ground was marked with footprints. The trees whispered in the courtyard and the mirrors in our rooms rippled when we ran past the open doors, and I thought I heard Neha giggle and dive into one of the rooms at the end of the east corridor. I sprinted across the courtyard, shouting her name. She giggled again and waved a spindly arm from the doorway. I reached the corridor and went in after her.

The room was empty – except for a large wet crow with a broken wing perched on the edge of the skylight. It watched me with red, beady eyes and shook raindrops off its feathers.

I whirled, taking in each corner. I remember feeling a sense of loss. Daylight was waning, and when I turned again it wasn't the room I'd entered. Instead of the sparse wooden charpoy there was a finely made bed with pillows and brocaded quilts, a sandalwood footstool placed at its end. A body-length mirror gleamed beside the bed. The walls were hung with canted paintings whose beauty, strangely, could not be admired: the moment I leaned in for a closer look, the pictures blurred.

I turned to look at the mirror. It was a fabulous piece of workmanship, its edges carved in mahogany with sparrows in flight. The girl in the mirror looked back at me with wide, black eyes. She couldn't have been more than my age. Her eyelids were swollen, her lips red, shaped like leaves felled by autumn rain. A bruise flowered from the root of her left ear, all the way up her scalp. She looked neither happy nor unhappy. A passing ghost, I thought, gone forever the moment I departed from this strange new room.

As I watched, the girl in the mirror leaned back, pointed at me and began to laugh. The sound filled the room, a cacophony of maddened birdsong. She laughed and laughed, and the air heated with her laughter, and the skylight darkened with night. A whoosh of blistering air, my nostrils filling up with a bitter smell like charred flesh or feathers, and the girl in the mirror was smoking. Coils of grey-black rose from her hair like braids. Smoke ringed her eyes, now orange-blue. She flapped her skinny, crinkling arms, and I cried out and turned, knocking over the footstool, and fled from the room.

Later, after I was calmed by Sangeeta Apa and Bibi Soraiya with hot tea and a thin slice of buttered bread, I told them about the room and its fiery inhabitant. Sangeeta Apa and Bibi glanced at each other.

'Was there a stove in the room?' Bibi Soraiya asked.

'I didn't see one,' I said.

She nodded. 'Go to your room, bachey. Shut the door and get some sleep. I'll tell your sisters not to bother you.'

Neha came to my bed that night. We were roommates, three of us, but our third was sick and they'd put her up in the east wing. 'What happened?' Neha asked, draping an arm across my body.

I told her. When I got to the part about following her into the room, her eyes widened, like the girl-in-the-mirror's had, and she began to breathe irregularly – an exacerbation of her asthma. We had to rush her to Mayo Hospital where the doctors made her spend that night and the night after.

To this day she insists that the girl with the spindly arm wasn't her. Neha was hiding atop one of the courtyard trees and showed me fresh scratches from the branches on her left arm. I believed her. I have always believed her.

That was the first time I saw a ghost in the orphanage. There were two more instances.

Both on the night before Sangeeta Apa's wedding dinner.

In story hour on a Friday, Sangeeta Apa told us the tale of the mythical bird huma. Persian legend holds, she said, that the huma never rests. It circles ceaselessly high above the earth, invisible to prisoners of earthly time, impervious.

Furthermore, they say (said Sangeeta Apa):

It eats bones. The female lays her eggs in the air. As the egg drops, the hatchling squirms out and escapes before the shell hits the earth. It is a bridge between the heavens and earth. It's a bird of fortune. The shadow of the huma falling on a man bequeaths royalty on his person. The huma once refused to travel to the far ends of the earth, for wherever its shadow fell the masses would become kings and the huma is very particular about bestowing kingship. Like the phoenix, it is old and deathless. In an alternate form, it has seen the destruction of the world three times over

and

it cannot be taken alive. Whosoever captures it will die in 40 days.

It is a story I have thought about many times since.

We were all in love with the bird man. Who wouldn't be?

Every evening he came cycling down Multan Road, trilling the bell on his bicycle, which was laden with birdcages and wicker baskets. The baskets brimmed with candles, lice combs, fans, attar bottles, incense and other household items. He was a short, thin man, and very clumsy – I can't tell you how many times we helped him pick up dropped merchandise, cages, even his turban. The turban was large and sequined with a starched turra at the top. Many times we saw him in clothes with holes in them – once he even circled the neighborhood barefoot – but we never saw that turra unstarched, even if his awkwardness meant we frequently glimpsed his long, beautiful, oiled hair, which would have suited our own heads so well, we thought.

The bird man would stop under a peepal tree near the entrance of the orphanage. Grinning, he'd get off the bicycle and spread a woollen shawl on the ground. He'd set his cages down and begin twittering. He could whistle, warble, chirrup, cheep and caw as well as any bird he carried, startling new customers and delighting old.

He followed this musical prologue with a show displaying his birds' impeccable training in divination.

The bird man sold all manner of birds: parrots, pigeons, bank mynahs, Australian lovebirds (his hottest item), but there were two he wouldn't part with – a pair of green rose-necked parakeets. These parakeets had mastered the art of soothsaying. They fluttered impatiently in a painted blue wooden cage, while the bird man fanned out a stack of white envelopes on the shawl. The envelopes had gilded borders, and soaring birds, their outline dulled by time and use, were embossed in the corners.

Curious customers, many of them prematurely aged women, would come up and look. Shy at first, they would gather courage, put out their hands for examination, and pose their questions:

Will I ever get married? Will my firstborn be a boy? Will that please my husband? My mother-in-law wants more dowry and loathes me. What should I do?

And

should I stay away from the gas stove in the kitchen?

We girls would gather around the bird man as he frowned and took their hands. His fingernails were long and manicured, and softly they traced the lines on the women's palms. He had a comforting smell about him, like earth, or bird, or the way my hands smelled after rolling dough peras on the nights it was my turn to bake rotis. He spoke gently to the women, whispering, calming their nerves.

Only then would he lift the door of the blue cage, letting one of the parakeets hop out.

The bird would pace back and forth across the envelopes. It nipped and pecked at them, its small head darting, until finally it gripped an envelope's edge. It would lift it in its beak and prop it against its emerald body. The bird man would take the envelope, extract the piece of paper inside, pop a tablet of sweet choori into the parakeet's beak, and read the prophecy to the wide-eyed customer.

He was never wrong, the women said. So many before him were charlatans, they said. Their eyes glowed when they said it, and the bird man's admirers grew and grew.

My sisters and I were his admirers as well. Sangeeta Apa would watch him from the entrance of the orphanage, the end of her cotton dopatta caught between her teeth. He would laugh with us and tell us our fortunes for free. Sometimes he teased Apa: 'Whomever you marry will become a king among men.' He would give us gifts: bird-shaped candles, vials of attar, bottles of scented oil. He was a good man, we thought. Wise and ageless.

Sometimes, after the Rishtay Wali Aunty had been by, we would ask him to tell us the would-be bride's future. Always he refused.

'Palm lines and the paths of heavenly bodies are malleable. Hard work, prayer, love – they can reshape them,' he would say. 'Take care of your new family and all will be well.'

We wanted to believe him and sometimes we did, but, even at that age, we knew better. The orphanage was our mother and father. Beyond its walls, who knew?

The walls of the orphanage were dun-coloured.

I remember this even if I have forgotten other things – the face of the old pastor who came tottering down the courtyard on Sundays; the smell of trees that lined the courtyard (which trees? I remember orange and red mulberry, but which at the courtyard's end by Sangeeta Apa's room – the tree that cast a long, shocked shadow?); the colour of the bird man's turban, the sequins of which flared red as he pedalled his bicycle down Multan Road at dusk. Strange how we drown in recollection at the least propitious of times but cannot pluck memories from the past's branches when we need them.

Sangeeta Apa.

No end or beginning to some tales, but the middle is always there. She was the middle of all our stories, the centre sitting still and sombre when everyone around her rode, quickly or sluggishly, the tide of time in the orphanage. Days and weeks and months and years – the Rishtay Wali Aunty's arrival marked them and whittled them away. Thirty-six girls of all ages. So many of my sisters came and went. So many marriages and migrations – yet Sangeeta Apa remained, braiding our hair, peeling mangoes, husking peas and walnuts, dyeing Bibi Soraiya's hair with henna (the smell of that henna, rich and secret, like a sunset glimpsed from a crevice under the canal bridges); and as we giggled and ran around the courtyard, singing songs,

We are a flock of sparrows, Father
One day we will fly away

Sangeeta Apa would shake her head and laugh, the sound ringing out loud and shrill and mysterious, until its final notes couldn't be told from the twilight birdsong.

It was a very long time before the Rishtay Wali Aunty came for her. By then Apa was in her 40s, half her head silvered with age.

I remember the day well because Mano was sick – he had been puking all morning. Red and black feathers glistened in the wedding cat's vomit. Bibi Soraiya fretted over him and fetched him digestive sherbet from the animal doctor three streets away, but Mano wouldn't touch it. Nor would he eat anything else. He just crawled across the courtyard and lay next to the entrance, waiting.

The Rishtay Wali Aunty arrived in a green-backed rickshaw. We were in class in the north corridor, and from the window I saw her dismount. A squat woman with one droopy eye and features hardened by time and sun, she waddled to the entrance and rang the bell. Bibi Soraiya appeared and opened the door. Together, they stepped over Mano, crossed the courtyard, and disappeared behind the thick line of trees in the direction of Bibi's quarters.

A good match had been found for Sangeeta Apa, we would later discover.

'The boy is 51 and very pious,' Bibi Soraiya told us the next day when we assembled in the courtyard to sing the national anthem. 'He lives in Gujranwala and owns a dairy shop. Your Apa is really lucky. His dowry demands are so reasonable.'

We whooped and cheered and congratulated Apa. She stood there, still as a lake, her gaze on the wedding cat, who was feeling better and kept walking between Apa's legs, mewling. The hem of Apa's dopatta crept into her mouth, and the din we made startled a host of sparrows that escaped, cheeping, into the sky.

That night I saw my second and third ghosts.

I was returning from the cigarette stall – Bibi Soraiya had a fondness for hookah and gave me a bar of Jubilee chocolate each time I fetched her tobacco. A clear night with a blue moon full as a houri's lips shining above the orphanage, and Mano was by the entrance, his tail twitching. I bent to scratch his chin. He slipped away, turned and watched me, eyes glinting like coins in the dark beneath the trees.

'You hungry? Want some milk, Mano-billi?' I said, patting my pocket to make sure the roll of tobacco hadn't fallen out.

The wedding cat purred. He arched his back, twisted, and started for the east corridor. He circled a (maple?) trunk, stopped, and looked back at me.

'What is it? Not feeling better?'

Mano gazed at me. Night dilated around us. The cat shivered and hissed, his tail puffing up, and lunged to the trees. I would have left him to whatever mischief he was up to and gone my way, but Mano had been acting odd all day. I called then dashed after him.

He was a blur in the blackness and sometimes he was a sound. I followed him to the edge of the east corridor where he waited, ears pinned back, pawing the ground before one of the rooms. He saw me and blinked.

The wedding cat went inside the room.

I glanced down the unlit corridor. Nothing moved through its length. No sounds. Not one rectangle of light stretched from open doorways, which seemed narrower and more numerous than I had ever seen.

I looked at the room Mano had entered. A peculiar effect of light and dark turned the framework of its door pale blue, as if a thin coating of paint had been applied to the wood. The doorway was wedged between Sangeeta Apa's room and another girl's whose name escapes me. Inside, silver light flickered. Shadows moved beyond a curtain of mist or smoke.

I mothed to the strange light and entered the room.

By this time I had been at the orphanage for a number of years and watched half a dozen of my sisters get married. Their ages ranged from 13 to 30. Out of the six, we escorted three to the train station and one to the bus. One disappeared, nobody knew where, and one was married to an elderly clerk in the local municipality office who was, happily, receptive to bribes from the needful. This man had thrived and could afford a lavish wedding in a real wedding hall – Lala's Shadi House near Data Darbar. My sisters and I, therefore, had occasion to put on our best dresses, and we danced and sang at the baaraat party to our heart's content. It remains one of my fondest memories.

The wedding hall I was in now made Lala's Shadi House seem like a shanty.

It was the grandest room I had ever seen or would see. Pentagonal in shape, flanked by pillared archways, it was strewn with rose petals at the entrance and the far end. Motia and bright feather wreaths decked the walls, as did colourful mosaics and tapestries (these blurred when I passed them so I could never make out the images). Persian rugs were arranged in geometric patterns on the floor and spiralling crystal chandeliers sparkled and glimmered overhead. Candelabras lined the walls and threw such a chiaroscuro of light and shadow that the rugs (so fine they felt like extensions of my skin) seemed to shift beneath my passage.

My memory of the room is perfect, so vivid that it still lives behind my eyelids. I can shut my eyes now and see everything in profuse detail.

At the far end of the room was a cage on a raised platform. A bridegroom and his bride sat cross-legged on an embellished takht inside it.

I walked forward. The groom wore a sherwani glittering with sequins, and garlands of red flowers and rupee notes around his neck. His face was covered with a veil of charred feathers. The woman wore a gold–red wedding dress and was laden with jewellery from head to toe. Wherever her skin was exposed, it was painted with henna. She was breathtaking.

Now I noticed other cages secreted away in arched recesses on either side of me. Silent men and women in colourful shalwar kurtas and saris sat inside on wooden perches and swings. Their eyes followed me as I moved down the hall. Their lips were parted. From each mouth protruded what I first thought were albino tongues. A second look dismissed the idea. The objects were pale and card-shaped.

Soundless, the doors of all cages slid up. The inmates rose and stepped outside.

I was surrounded by the wedding procession now. My nostrils filled with a smell as organic as it was old.

In a flurry of blue and green and black we marched to the couple's cage. Their door swung open, revealing a three-step deck carpeted with red feathers and fall leaves. The crowd surged forward, elbow to elbow, carrying me on its breast. Their footfall was perfectly silent. I couldn't even hear their breathing.

We halted before the stage.

Two men in crow-black swept across the hall, up the stair deck, into the cage. They held a bowl of milk. The bridegroom swung his veil of burnt feathers aside and sipped. The crow men presented the bowl to the bride. She dipped her head coyly (but not before I saw that her eyes were large and different-coloured) and drank until the man gently removed the bowl from her lips and placed it on the step deck.

Mano the wedding cat appeared from behind the stage. He sauntered up the steps and began to lap up the remaining milk. Come to me, Mano, I tried to say, but the words wouldn't leave my lips. Satiated, Mano yawned, licked his haunches and started circling the wedding cage.

A woman in all white with a birthmark beneath her left eye was beside me. She was built like a briefcase, short and squat and business-like. She gazed at me for a moment and pointed at the ceiling.

I looked up.

The hall's ceiling was covered in the fresco of a giant

bird. The bird was perfectly captured in mid-flight, its golden-dark serrated wings scything a blue sky. It had a rainbow plumage, black horns and a peacock tail. Glinting feathers, like embers, showered from its underbelly. In the flickering light, the painting appeared to cast a vast shadow over the proceedings.

I lowered my gaze and the woman was gone. In her place was one of the crow men. Gray sparrows sat on his shoulders and pecked at his hair. He held out an enamel basin in front of him. Liquid sloshed inside; its vapours made my eyes water.

The crow man bowed and began walking to the wedding cage.

Now excited chittering rose as the guests removed the card-like objects from their mouths and showered the wedding couple with them. Prayers, cheers, shouts and the wailing of women overcome by the prospect of a daughter's separation mounted, until you couldn't tell if the processionists were celebrating or mourning.

Mubarak! Mubarak! Be blessed in your husband's house.

May you never have cause to leave that home. May you never be short of dowry.

May your firstborns be healthy baby boys.

May your mother-in-law never hate you.

May you never return to your parents. Should you return, come only as a dead body

and

may you stay safe from the stove, the stove, the stove!

Now burst the wedding songs from a hundred throats, ancient, powerful, loving, imprisoning, humiliating; and the crow man walked. He walked towards the bride with the basin of slopping liquid that gave off fumes.

She sat in her cage, placid as the sea, ageless like a vow unfulfilled. Only when the man reached her and doused her in the vaporous liquid did she stir. Her jewels slid and chinked. The tapestries on the walls darkened. The groom's veil of charred feathers dropped from his head, and the red of the bride's dress deepened until it turned a perfect black.

The procession rejoiced.

May you stay safe from the stove!

Mano was between my legs. The wedding cat flicked his tail and tripped me. I flailed my arms, stumbled and when I looked up, the wedding hall was gone. The cages, the guests, the beautiful bride with her splendid mismatched eyes (which I have seen in dream many times since), the elegant ornamentation – all vanished.

Just an orphan's room, empty of poise or promise.

I was afraid. I wasn't afraid. I went back to the courtyard and looked at the sky. So many stars that night, and the blue moon, it watched the world as it always had. A bulbous bird staked to the heavens, it spread its vast gaze over all our affairs. Its eye was filled with something deep and raw. Now when I close my eyes and imagine that moon, I think what I saw was mystery and memory and a longing so old it makes me shudder.

My cheeks were wet. I went to deliver the tobacco (still in my pocket) and as I passed Sangeeta Apa's door, the sounds of hushed conversation came, as did soothing odours of incense, earth and rubbing oil. When I returned from Bibi Soraiya's quarters, Sangeeta Apa's door was ajar. Leaves rustled. I glanced up to see a figure, bulky, as if with a thick garment, clinging to the tree (which tree?) outside her room.

The moon fled behind a cloud. When it returned, the ghostly figure was gone.

The wedding dinner was short and sweet. There was biryani, sweet lassi, mangoes and lychees (it was summer). Rumours of silver-papered firni-in-jotas from Gawal Mandi floated for a while before Bibi Soraiya dismissed them.

The groom was a looming, forbidding man who bowed his head again and again and made squeezing gestures with his fists when too many of my sisters crowded him. Sangeeta Apa and he wore matching wedding outfits. She wouldn't look at him, but peeked from behind her ghoongat, smiling, when Neha and I tried to steal his brown leather shoes – Joota Chupai is an accepted custom. Bibi Soraiya yelled at us and we reluctantly returned them.

They left for Gujranwala the next day by train.

I have not seen nor heard of my Sangeeta Apa since. If she called or wrote letters, Bibi Soraiya didn't tell us, which was strange because my others sisters stayed in touch for a few years, at least, before life overtook them. The unsettling shadow of Apa's absence grew, but even after I was all grown up, if I asked about her, Bibi's eyes would change. With age, Bibi developed a tremor in her face and limbs, and mere mention of Apa would send her shaking to bed. It got so bad that I stopped asking.

In the ensuing years, Neha and many of my other sisters were married off. Sorted out, arranged and packed away. Bus stops with their tang of sweat and diesel on your tongue. Train stations odorous with dust and cheap perfume and the ashy smell of sparks from rail tracks. Young girls appeared and replaced my sisters – a ceaseless commotion of laughs and shouts and dopattas flying in the courtyard wind. I loved them all, but, bless my memory, I remember few. Sometimes when I peered at their faces, it seemed as if their features blurred and ran together and one familiar mask emerged, winter breath rising from its lips like smoke. When that happened, I would get up and walk to the entrance of the orphanage. I would stand there and watch the world beyond those walls, an unfettered landscape widening away beyond the limits of my vision. Somewhere out there, I thought, you didn't need to be wedded to resignation or despair. There was stuff in between. Hearths instead of stoves. If you got too warm, you could step away. You could leave. You didn't have to leave. You didn't have to fear leaving, or falling, or ceaselessly circling and not ever coming to rest.

You could travel to the ends of the earth. You didn't have to fear remembering.

By then I was busy helping Bibi run the orphanage; I had to put such thoughts out of my head. Still, I sometimes dreamed. Of discomfiting things that became grainy, wispy echoes in the morning. Crossroads with signs askew pointing this way and that; graveyards planted next to wedding halls; windows that shuttered open and closed; doorways that led to more doorways, their gaping mouths atremble with flickering light; and in the distance, always, the flutter of dark wings. I would wake from these dreams with my fists darkened by sweat and dust, the taste of smoke already fading from my tongue.

The bird man still visited. He crouched on his shawl and twittered and chirped and spread the gilded envelopes, waiting for his parakeets to tell his admirers' fortunes. May be I was getting old or he, but his bird music seemed duller to me, as if his voice had aged. Once he came inside the orphanage to talk to Bibi Soraiya about something and my sisters gathered around him. I sat and watched him play to the girls. He turned his head from side to side. His turban fell off. I picked it up and handed it to him.

'Thank you,' he said, dusting it with his large earthy hand. 'Sometimes I wonder if it's time to take this off for good.'

'Why?'

'Vanity be damned, it's just an old turban, you know.' He laughed, a loud, booming sound that startled me. 'One can dream, but that won't change it into a crown.' His eyes looked a little feverish. He said, 'You know sparrows are a delicacy in Gujranwala. They trap dozens in nets and roast them slow on large stoves. My father used to go eat there with friends once in a while, but my mother would get angry. She said the poor things had no meat on them at all and it was a sin to take so many tiny lives for nothing.'

I must have frowned, or my face lost colour, for he changed the subject. Shortly after, he left.

The oddest thing I remember after Apa's departure?

Exactly 40 days after Bibi took her to the train station, all the birds, the silent birds, the soaring, splendid birds that came to us from every corner of Lahore, stopped visiting. The courtyard trees grew heavy with unpecked fruit, the electric poles became forlorn. Long after they vanished, the courtyard remained filled with the rich, old smell of bird. (These days, the odour makes me break out in a sweat.)

And in our rooms the mirrors rippled and moonlight changed and people from the past walked restlessly back and forth between places of someone else's making.

DEAD LOVERS ON EACH BLADE, HUNG

J*ee Inspector Sahib.*

He came looking for a missing girl in Lahore Park one evening in the summer of 2013; this man known as Hakim Shafi. It was a summer to blanch the marrow of all summers. Heat rose coiling like a snake from the ground. Gusts of evil loo winds swept across Lahore from the west, shrinking the hides of man and beast alike, and Hakim Shafi went from bench to bench, stepping over needles in bleached June grass, and showed the heroinchies a picture.

Have you seen this girl, he said.

For all his starched kurta shalwar and that brown waistcoat, his air was neither prideful nor wary. He was a very tall, bony man with stooped shoulders, a ratlike face and thick whiskers. His eyes were sinkholes that bubbled occasionally, and when we said no, we hadn't seen that girl, Shafi's gaze drifted away from the benches, the park and the night sky.

We distrusted him. This lost stranger – we had no doubt he was lost – we watched wander the park for weeks. Each Friday he came after juma prayers, that coloured eight-by-six photo clasped between his palms, as if the girl in the floral-patterned shalwar kameez and his prayers were intertwined. Before I knew that they were, I laughed with the others at his inquiries. It was amusing to see this well dressed gentleman court our company, eyes full of hope, that faded picture in his hands.

In his absence, we speculated. He looked in his 50s, may be early 60s. Perhaps the girl was his runaway daughter. As we injected the queen into our veins, as we gave ourselves up to dreaming in her orbit, we argued whether the rich-born pretty girl with her sad eyes and smooth skin was roughing it out with lowlifes, while her father searched for her in the shadows. We giggled when we thought of that.

You understand how our life is, sahib, don't you? We heroinchies are the children of the white queen – a tribe unto ourselves. We do not share space with the outside; our years pass differently in her presence. Hers is a shadow that enwombs us: It nurtures us as it suffocates – it is a bit like being slowly, sinuously lowered into an endless grave and watching that dome of light shrink until its memory becomes hateful. You fall in love with the descent.

With Hakim Shafi things might have gone on that way – he on his insoluble quest and we daytiming when we could – but Mustafa, our dealer, he got greedy and fucked up everything. I have wished upon my dead father's name many times for that bastard Mustafa to rot in hell. Had he not ruined it for all of us, I would not be sitting here tonight with you and the sub-inspector sahib in this skeleton of a police station with its shadow-draped oil lamps and broken windows and sweat-slick bars. In this stench of metal and piss and—

No, sahib, it's not like that. Just saying greed is the most dangerous of beasts, as my old Dada used to say, and Mustafa's stupid greed dragged us into the darkness that finally showed its teeth tonight.

So this is what happened with that son of a whore Mustafa.

Before he came along, we used to get our masala behind the flower market in Liberty; a paan-and-cigarette stall owner was our man. His crop was fresh and as pure as any Lahori queen has ever been. It was expensive, but we made do by snatching cellphones, stealing manhole covers and hubcaps, rummaging through garbage for sellables and begging. Most of us could snag two or three hits a week. Wasn't much, but was enough to keep the night time at bay.

Then came news that in Kunar Afghan police had set hundreds of thousands of poppy fields ablaze. Overnight, opium supply dropped. As the Pakistani Army's battle against militants up north intensified, prices shot up, and we found every door shut and bolted on us with nothing but the habit to keep us company. Such desperate times that many of us became cotton shooters and fluffers. Chicken shit, I know, but what could you do? There was only so much queen to go around.

'I know a man who knows a man,' said Yasin one day. Five of us were crouched around a bench under the oldest peepal tree in the park, and Yasin, a scrawny lizard-like heroinchi who had recently turned to fluffing, sat grinding milk-sugar and a laxative he stole from a dispensary to bulk up our meagre supply. 'He can get us cheap masala.'

'Nothing is cheap,' someone said and gawked at the blue velvet of the evening sky.

'It's that or we are dry. I'm completely out.'

Nothing we could say to this. Enter Shani, Yasin's man's man.

He was a fidgety midget with a wispy mustache wider than his face and he offered to help us ride the queen cheap. Word was that he had made deals with police stations in Model Town and Kot Lakhpat for confiscated masala and knew how to tap into the Army's black market—

Yes, sahib, of course, you're right. The bastard was likely lying all along.

Suffice to say he knew people, and so we eagerly accepted. I was among those who stopped going to the flower market and trusted this fiend for my needs.

As you can see, that was a mistake. My dying is ample evidence of that.

It happened on a Thursday evening. (I remember because one of the heroinchies went to Data Sahib's shrine to pay his respects.) After the park guard made his rounds to collect bhatta for letting us use the benches, most of my group left to polish-wipe cars and beg at traffic lights. Seemed as good a time as any to retrieve the plastic-wrapped masala I had squirrelled away weeks ago. I pulled out the packet and rolled up my sleeves and, under the swaying elms and peepal, I slipped the queen into my blood.

(Yes, sub-inspector sahib, that cigarette is most welcome. Thank you for the light. This close the flame hurts my eyes a bit, but my hands are shaking and I cannot chase the dragon at this hour.)

Sahib, we sit here today in this gloomy thana. I can plainly see the shadows squirm by the door, the oak and eucalyptus boughs moving in the wind. Hear that whistle in the dark outside. Watch the way your fingers wind the ends of your mustache, your eyes half-lidded as you listen to my story. I smell the ash falling to the floor from the tip of my cigarette. See water bead on the plastic sheet over that ice block the sub-inspector wheeled in earlier, should I prove less than cooperative – and I swear on my mother's name, this is how clearly I saw my dead son under those wheezing trees that night.

Heroinchies die twice, they say, and we can all remember the story of our first death.

My son is mine.

He was 12 when I beat him black and blue on his

birthday. He wanted to enroll in school again; I wanted him to train as a mechanic's apprentice. He was 13 when he ran away, and 15 when they found him in a gunnysack behind a dumpster at Lakshmi Chowk. His face was swollen and discoloured in a dozen places. His lips were torn. Blood had clotted in the corners.

His throat—

His throat was—

I died the day they found him, sahib, and I died again that night in the park after I injected the masala. And in this fresh death when my son came to me he was smooth and untouched. Angelic was my boy. He bent over me and I thought he had forgotten, that he had forgiven. His eyes were kind. He smiled at me, changing, and it wasn't his face but a piss-coloured full moon shining at me. The eyes were red stars, the darkness between them whipped out and licked my cheeks. The white queen was in a mood, she rose with the tide of my blood, and I saw a giant golden snake tower above me. Its hood pulsated wider than the night sky until it seemed the heavens stood on its flared head, and I knew, I was sure, that its basilisk gaze would be my end.

The world shivered and came apart. A gaunt man with a bristling mustache leaned across the bench, his hands poised above my chest. He lowered his face, breath afoul with onion, garlic, something else, and said, Are you all right?

I was.

Later, Hakim Shafi would tell me that I was gone. When he found me, head lolling off the bench, my mouth frothed and my eyes were glazed. The left side of my body twitched. When he found no pulse, he pumped my chest and continued for nearly 15 minutes. That was how long I was dead, he said.

I believed him. How else could I have seen my son in that gloaming?

Hakim Shafi saved my life that night. A medical man present at that hour in a corner of a park haunted by heroinchies – some might call that a divine act. May be it was, but I wonder. Sometimes I think life is like a junkie's flesh, criss-crossed where kismet injects other souls into our lives. Souls lost as we are. Who knows if the perpetrator of such accidents is God or the devil?

Whatever force it was, it bound my life to Hakim Shafi's forever.

'I'm fine,' I said, but he brought me to his small, neat clinic in Old Lahore anyway. Here, he drew my blood and took a pinch of the leftover masala for testing. We sat on a moss-coloured couch and watched the powder bubble and hiss in a glass vial when Hakim poured acid on it.

'Look at the bottom,' he said. I looked. Molten black residue, like tar, stuck to the glass. 'Your dealer's been short-changing you,' he said. 'I'd guess for a while, too. Elephant tranquilizer. This heroin has more cut in it than any I have seen. It was just a matter of time before something happened.'

I nodded, and it occurred to me I was a bit disappointed. I had been courting my demise for a long while.

'You inject.' It wasn't a question. I nodded again. He touched the spectacles he had put on inside the clinic. They made him look confused. He dragged his knuckles back and forth on the oak desk. 'You get your blood tested for hepatitis?'

'No.'

'You know how to chase the dragon? May be that's the way to go if you can't kick the habit.'

'What makes you think I want to kick anything?'

Hakim Shafi pulled at a drawer and brought out four tiny vials. He picked up the syringe cocked with my blood, and dropped some in each vial.

My mind was fogged up from my death. I wanted to rise and flee to the park, but Shafi's eyes were fixed on me. Restless, I scanned the room and saw a framed picture on the desk. I pointed. 'That your daughter?'

Shafi's fingers whitened around the vial. He shook it vigorously. 'Did you eat today?'

'I've seen you take that picture around the park. I know everyone's told you she was never there.'

Shafi flicked a finger against the glass. The yellow liquid turned red then golden. 'I'll set up some intravenous saline for you. Your blood is thick from fluid loss.'

He helped me on to the couch and gave me a concoction to drink. When my eyelids grew heavy, he pulled a crisp white sheet over me. It smelled of hospitals.

'Sleep well. It's the only way most of us can dream.' He paused, and in the silence a drowsy moth thunked against the room's window. I muttered. Somewhere in the night a baby cried, and its mother shushed it and began to hum. The moth thunked again. I looked, and outside the window, a small boy-shape pressed its face against the glass, mouthing words at me.

'Hakim sahib,' I said, voice thick and sticky. 'Who's that?'

Shafi turned. The shape was gone.

In a room at the back of the clinic, Hakim Shafi showed me snake skins.

'This is how I make my living.'

'By killing snakes?'

He smiled. 'By using venom to heal. *Similia similibus curantur.*' He swept a hand around him at the hundreds of glass vials, filled with pills the size of sugar cubes, arranged on dusty shelves. 'Like cures like. Poison will kill poison.' He knuckled the diamond-patterned leathery skin. 'My suppliers send me tokens every year. Skins, fangs, vertebra. Keeps up the clinic's image. Helps the business.'

I scratched the stubble on my chin. 'How does snake venom heal? I thought the only thing it was useful for was killing dumb assholes who mess around with creatures they don't understand.'

'Truly it's one of the oldest cures. My ancestors have used it for centuries.'

'You're pulling my chain, aren't you, Hakim sahib?'

Shafi gave me a look. 'We're so besieged by newness we forget old diseases haunt us for a reason. Did you know snake venom is being researched at big universities these days? Dementia, palsy, heart attacks – it has a role in curing all of them.' He went to a cupboard and pulled down a large rosewood box from the top shelf. He set it on the table next to a gleaming row of vials and tubes. 'For my medicines, I mix most of the substrate myself. The venom varies between species. Some is toxic to human nerves, some to blood, some to tissues and organs. A pinch of the wrong sample, and you'd be dead in seconds.'

He opened the rosewood box. Inside were dozens of matchbook-sized tins. He pulled on a pair of gloves and carefully removed the lids of two. They were filled with tiny snow-coloured pellets.

'This,' Shafi picked up a pellet with a pair of tweezers, 'is the venom of the common krait. It paralyzes the breathing muscles. If you get bitten by a krait during sleep, you'd scratch the spot, thinking it was a bug bite, and doze off. You'd never wake again.' He replaced the pellet in the tin. 'I use it for patients with lockjaw and neck spasms. A millionth portion in goat milk. Highly effective.'

He tapped another tin with the edge of his tweezers. 'A couple bring their nine-year-old girl to me every month. She has thin blood. A genetic condition. Bleeds for hours from her gums if she brushes her teeth too vigorously. A knee scrape would be fatal. Most children like her don't survive childhood. My Koriwala viper venom has kept her alive for seven years.'

I shuddered. My third day at the clinic, and the shakes were beginning to hit me. My skin itched with strange life. I felt it in the bunching of my bowels, at the back of my eyes. The absence of the queen was becoming loud and insistent.

I licked my lips. 'Got anything to help my nerves, Hakim sahib?'

Shafi tipped his neck and watched me. He plucked a vial filled with russet-coloured liquid from the shelf. 'Cobra in laudanum. It will help the diarrhoea and muscle aches.' When I eyed it warily, he laughed. 'Diluted. Don't worry. I know what I'm doing.'

He shook the vial, dipped a glass pipette into the frothing liquid, and retrieved some. I opened my mouth and he squeezed three drops on to my tongue.

'Easy,' he said when I rolled my tongue around. 'Let it settle into your tissues.'

Already, the fire in my body was sputtering, calming down. It wasn't the queen's embrace, but it was something. When I closed my eyes, a fog rose and surrounded me, whispering me into a lull.

By now, sahib, you must be wondering why I was still at the clinic with the good hakim – why I stayed for weeks and didn't steal his medicines, his laudanum or his money. For years, since my boy died and my wife ran away with a shakarkandi vendor, I had done nothing but steal. Hubcaps, tin sheets, tools from a garage where I worked briefly, an old beggar's wheelchair – you name it.

Before I became a thief, I worked in a dispensary – a tiny roadside stall in Qila Gujjar Singh run by a compounder named Ram Lal. He mixed tonics for common illnesses. Occasionally, a government doctor would check in, but mostly Ram Lal was free to do as he pleased. He was a good compounder, even though he did not have a medical degree. He helped the locals and earned a good name for himself with his gentle manner and willingness to subsidize his prescriptions.

I helped him run the dispensary. I attended seven grades before I dropped out of school and could read labels written in English on pill bottles. My job was to grind pills with a mortar and pestle and wrap them in squares of newspaper to make medicinal puris. We did well and it was a good life – until my son disappeared.

I suppose being in a similar environment with Hakim Shafi brought back those memories. For years I lived in that park – scabies-infested, filthy, often hungry. I had grown addicted to the darkness, but I suppose I was ready for it to end when I overdosed. Shafi came along, saved me, cleaned me up, and I guess I was just too sick of myself to rob him. I don't know, may be every heroinchi also wants one story with a happy ending.

Shafi helped me through the next week. Quitting cold turkey was like being cooked on a spit. I ground my teeth, I writhed and screamed, but his tinctures helped. I suspect he could have done more, but he knew this was my battle, and would only go so far in steering. The ship and its course were mine and mine alone.

Like cures like, he'd said.

On the seventh day, when I had more strength, Shafi showed me the terrariums.

His clinic was located in Old Lahore. Squeezed between a shoemaker's shop and a cloth merchant's, it was more like Ram Lal's dispensary than a real clinic. His patients came in lines of worn, sickly faces, most of them women and children. They crowded into the dingy waiting room up front where whorls of Quranic calligraphy draped the walls and the smell of formalin and bitter salts hung in the air.

When I had enough vigour to navigate past the front hall to the backyard, the fierce, sudden beauty of it shocked me. A statuary of ceramic children laughing and kneeling in the mud stood in the centre of a lush zoysia grass patch. Creepers hung from trestles arrayed across carrot patches, weaving between the half-dozen mango and orange trees that circled the statuary. Exquisitely kept and trimmed, the yard smelled of citrus and honeysuckle.

I whistled when Shafi told me he did the landscaping himself. 'That's hard work.'

He nodded. 'My wife helped me do it. She was a wonder.'

'Was?'

'Yes.'

I turned to a row of empty glass tanks in a corner of the yard. 'What are those?'

'Terrariums.' He crouched and ran a hairy hand over them. Monsoon season was upon us and night drizzle had left the glass shiny and clean. It twinkled in the afternoon light, slanting red shadows across the grass.

'You kept snakes?'

'My wife did. She was a herpetologist at the University of Punjab. Russell vipers, sand boas, Indian kraits, striped keelbacks – she kept them, fed them like babies.' He showed me cracks, little spiderwebs, in the glass. 'This is where her cobras tried to bite my hand.'

'What happened?' I said. Shafi yanked a tall weed poking its head from between the cages. We both knew I wasn't asking about snakes.

'I sold them,' he said. 'Couldn't bear to look at them any more.'

A thought hit me, a realization that must have shown in my face, for Shafi's eyes changed. He rose and retreated into the house, his footsteps impressed on the muddy banks of the flowerbeds, a trail leading into his past.

I got up to follow, then went to the back wall. I stooped and fingered the human footprint under the windowsill. It was fresh and clear and a child's. The toe prints were filled with rainwater.

A worm snaked its way out of a toe print and began wriggling madly in the rain pool.

The girl in the picture was not Hakim Shafi's daughter.

It was his wife – his child bride.

Shafi listened to my conclusion. I ran my fingers across the picture, across the large black eyes gazing out at the world, the nose proud, chin firm and defiant. The girl, in her early twenties, sat sidelong, a half-smile covered by a hennaed hand. With the nose ring, her broad forehead, and those eyes, she reminded me of desert women from Thal and Cholistan, who meander with their tribes across the wasteland, grazing cattle and weaving camel wool blankets.

I said as much to Shafi. He said, 'Eighteen years ago, I was in Hyderabad for a relative's funeral. I bought her from a band of gypsies who camped at the outskirts of the city. She was eight at the time.'

'Eight.' I was not shocked. I come from a family of moonshiners and shanty-dwellers, sahib. My father ran errands for a pimp most of his life. I knew how some old customs work. 'You raised your wife,' I said to him.

'Yes.'

I stared at the picture. 'Where is she now?'

Shafi polished a row of bottles with a rag.

'Why do you keep returning to the park?'

His voice was low. 'Maliha loved the park. She used to feed those stupid ducks at the pond. Loved their ugly dirt-coloured feathers. She said they reminded her of the desert. I used to laugh at that.' He yanked out a drawer and removed a brown pouch, its top cinched by leather thongs. From the pouch he took out and unwrapped a ball of paper, revealing a necklace strung with three large stones. They were cracked and yellow. 'These are the bones of her childhood.'

'What?'

'Desert pearls. Sandstone baked by heat for years. Maliha didn't remember much of her early life. Her parents were dead; there were tensions in the tribe – which is why they wanted to sell her to someone willing to take care of her. But she said she remembered her mother giving her these. Her mother told her they had magical powers and would protect her from jinns.' He smiled. 'My Maliha believed it till the day she disappeared.'

'When did she disappear?'

'Two years ago.'

'How old was she?'

'Twenty-six.'

'You loved her?'

It was a stupid question, sahib, I know, but asking it came so naturally, it surprised me. May be it was a bond of understanding between sinners. I could see his love for her nestled in the crowfeet around his eyes, I could see his entire life in those eyes: feeding her, clothing her, raising her, falling in love with her, sending her to college. But he had bought her with rupee. Her heart – did he win it, or chain it with need?

Shafi held the necklace. 'Yes, I loved her.'

'You didn't have children?'

'We were barren. I was.'

'Why did she run away?' I didn't mean to say what I said next, but I said it, 'A younger lover?'

His fingers pressed the stones as if telling beads on a rosary. 'She loved me. It might have been a mixed kind of love, but she did. I've always known that. She went away because she was looking for something. A dream. Something she heard when she was a child.' He brought the necklace close, until it brushed his chin. 'Many times, I thought she didn't know what she was looking for, but she was a precocious girl – always had been – and I trusted her.'

We were sitting at the table in the clinic's little kitchenette. Shafi got up and poured us green tea from a boiling pot. The scent of it drifted between us, sweet, spectral, ephemeral.

'Sometimes I feel her in the house, breathe her perfume. She left this necklace behind, you know.'

'And that has you convinced she'll return?'

He sipped tea.

'What was the dream she chased?'

'I don't know. The idea's a little insane, if I'm to be completely honest.'

'What was it?'

He put the cup down, shook his head. 'Not now. Another day, perhaps.'

Sahib, you might wonder why was he telling me all this. Why a respectable man like him would open his heart to a stranger, a heroinchi? I wondered the same, so I asked him.

He wrapped the necklace with the sheet and paper and placed it in the pouch. When he turned, his face was inscrutable. It comes out at last, I thought. No one is so good, so pious, so selfless that they'll pick up a dying needler from the garbage heap and take him home.

'I want your help,' Hakim Shafi said. His gray eyes were feverish. 'I want you to help me find my wife.'

'How could I? I haven't left that park in years.'

'Maliha disappeared from *that* park. I know it in my gut.'

I watched him. If his wife did visit her precious duck pond, I never saw her. Then again, in the darkness in which I thrived, she could have danced around me naked and I might have missed her.

He persisted, 'I want you to ask your friends. They won't tell me anything, but they will tell you. Someone must have seen her.' His hand trembled and tea spilled on the table. He wiped it with his sleeve. 'I've looked for her for two years now. I have talked to the police, and they've done nothing. They—' He stopped, clenched his fingers. 'Will you ask your friends? Please?'

I took another look at his face and I relented, sahib. God help me, I told him I would.

There are days when I wonder if I should have refused, if I should have got up and left his clinic and walked away fast as I could. In the end, I didn't. Not because he saved my life – I owe him no debt for that; he saved me to answer his own needs, I think – but because I had nothing to return to. The world is big, yes, but I had my own ghosts chasing me, and if I left, they'd just catch up sooner. Also, Shafi's love was naked and trembling, pinned to the wall. He was asking me to help him take it down, and I couldn't refuse.

I told him I'd ask around.

When I began my inquiry, Yasin – I believe I mentioned him before – directed me to some of the heroinchies who kept an eye on the goings-on in the park. One of them told me that two years ago, around the time Hakim Shafi's wife disappeared, the qawwals were in town.

Every year, a band of musicians comes to Lahore Park to take part in a qawwali festival. They're led by a maestro named Tariq Khan.

Yasin has a stereo he salvaged from a junkyard. When he shot up, he would often listen to Nusrat Fateh Ali Khan, his head thrashing to the alaap and raags. Occasionally I'd join him. Khan sahib's love songs are great, but we especially adored the ones that lauded the merits of sin. Whenever the qawwals came to town, we had front row seats to the free performances in the park.

I have not heard Tariq Khan sing, but legend says, when he was a young man, he was visited by the legendary Tansen in a dream and trained by him. That, at the peak of his prowess, Tariq Khan once set a dozen candles alight just with his singing.

'I saw her twice,' said Yasin's heroinchi confidante. 'A young woman hovering around the maestro Tariq Khan. Lovely girl. Beautiful dark eyes.'

When I prodded, his description of the girl matched Maliha's. The coincidence was too big to ignore. I asked Yasin to talk to the festival organizers, and he returned and told me that after each performance in Lahore, the qawwals left for Panjnad in southern Punjab. Perhaps Hakim Shafi could learn more if he visited the area?

I told Shafi.

At first he was incredulous, then his eyes widened. 'Ya Allah.' He wheeled and, ignoring my startled face, ran to his room and locked the door. I waited in the kitchenette for nearly an hour before he emerged.

'I know where she is,' he said.

'What? How?'

Shafi wiped a callused hand across his pale face. His fingers were grimy. 'Her family, her people – they were gypsy singers. They came from a lineage of "professional mourners": folks who'd come at the bidding of rich families to wail at funerals. To add glamour to their dead, so outsiders would think the departed was dearly beloved. Maliha would feel right at home with qawwals and their lyrical lamentations.' Shafi turned and stared out the window. 'At first I thought she went looking for her people. But she wouldn't do that. She wouldn't leave me for her folks. They sold her. She hated them for it. She'd never say it out loud – she wasn't one for self-pity – but I knew it.' His forehead creased and he talked in a low voice, as if to himself, 'No, she went looking for the naag mani. That's the only explanation.'

'Naag mani?'

'She's gone looking for her childhood.' Shafi turned his strange-coloured eyes on me. Nightfall was at hand, behind him the window was darkening, and I thought I saw something pale and glistening peer in. Shafi coughed and threw something across the table.

I looked down. It was his wife's necklace with the three desert stones.

'She's gone to Panjnad,' Shafi said, 'looking for the mythical serpent pearl.'

This is how Hakim Shafi gave away his life: First, he closed his shop. Next, he sold his house.

'What in the name of God are you doing?' I said.

Shafi grinned. 'Burning bridges,' he said.

I looked at him closely. In the four weeks since I'd told him about the qawwals, he had shaved his thick mustache and lost 10 kilos. He'd always been thin, but now he looked like a needler at the end of his days. His temples were wasted, the flesh of his face pulled taut across the blades of his bones. The grey in his eyes swirled madly, like smoke from charred moths after they crash into candles and explode into flame. It was as if a light had flicked on inside Shafi's head, bathing his body in an otherworldly glow whose secrets only he understood.

To be honest, I was becoming rather afraid of this skeletal man, sahib. I decided it was time for me to return to my world. Leave the clinic and flee to the park.

Which was when I discovered the true extent of the damage that motherfucker Mustafa, Yasin's dealer, had wrought.

We'd thought Mustafa had cut heroin deals with police stations only. Turned out he went a lot further than that.

He swindled the Poison Men themselves.

I don't know who came up with that name. When the opium fields up north were razed, people besides the militants lost a lot of money too. Folk with international connections – to whom many body bags in Lahore and Karachi were attributed.

Mustafa had been stealing the white queen from these people. Deep in his greed, he told the Poison Men his clientele was the city's elite; that we, the park heroinchies, were suppliers for children of bureaucrats and feudal lords.

Cunningly, he plotted it all out so that *we* became the swindlers and betrayers.

As they say, though, no one plots better than God. The Poison Men discovered that Mustafa was lying. He had been selling the queen and its substrate masala to their direct competitors in the international market.

Mustafa and his affiliates went missing.

Five of my friends paid the price for their greed as well. Yasin was among them. Their bodies were found in the pond near the banyan trees in the park, throats cut from ear to ear, rusted needles jammed inside their penises. Their fish-nibbled fingers – what few were left – were trapped in tree roots.

Word was that I was on their kill list as well. Me and some others. We were condemned. Dead men walking.

So, I resolved to stay missing. Hakim Shafi had made preparations to journey to the town of Uch, close to Panjnad, where, he had learned, the qawwals had gone. I begged to join him, and he was happy to have my company. He was expecting me to go with him all along, he said.

At noon, we got off the train at Bahawalpur Station and Hakim rented a taxi that would take us to Uch – a three-hour road trip.

On the way, he told me how he finally realized his wife's destination.

'As a child, Maliha used to talk about a mythical stone. She called it *naag mani*. A precious stone gifted by the Serpent King, who rules the underworld, to his queen.'

I stared at him. He didn't look like he was joking. 'And you think your wife went after this magic rock a snake gave his begum as a wedding present?'

Shafi guffawed as if it were the funniest thing in the world. His eyes were too bright. 'Why wouldn't she?' He chewed at his lip. 'Her people came from the desert. Her mother gave her that sandstone necklace and told her it would keep jinns away. There are stories of such stones in every culture.'

'Hakim sahib, that is insane. I thought she was an educated woman.'

He lifted his chin and stroked his throat. 'I have been thinking about this for a while, you know. She likely came up with rational reasons to justify her quest. I suspect she talked herself into looking for it. You're still sniffing and shaking your head.' He reached into his pocket, brought out his wife's necklace pouch, and unfolded the wrapping paper. 'I should have thought of it much sooner, but—'

'This is a copy of a letter she wrote to a herpetologist in America.'

I took the note and tried to read it. The English vocabulary was beyond me. Shafi saw me squinting and took it back. He read it and translated it for me.

Incidentally, it is the same note, sahib, that you retrieved from the rosewood box later. There, sub-inspector sahib, that's the one. If you like, you can read it yourself.

No? I see. It is to be part of my testimony. Well, I will tell you what I remember.

(*Item #13 pertaining to Case 546D3: Copy of letter from one Maliha Shafi, Evidence Collection Lab, Lahore*)

Dear Professor Hensoldt,

I have read with great interest your article about the Cobra Stone in the *New York Times* and was fascinated by your description of the hours you spent watching cobras catch fireflies in the grass.

You state that the female *lampyridae* has rudimentary wings and is too large to fly; that it sits in the grass quietly, emitting a green light stronger than the male's. The light flickers intermittently, and if watched for a long time 'a steady current of male insects will be observed flying toward it and alighting in close proximity' for mating.

You state that little pebbles of chlorophane emit a similar greenish light in the dark. It is possible, you say, that thousands of years ago, the cobra chanced upon such a stone in a riverbed and, thinking it a glow-worm, swallowed it. It then discovered the stone could be used to lure male fireflies. That, over millennia, the cobra has come to use the stone as decoy in the grass, and when the male insect weaves its way toward the stone's light, the snake lunges and catches it.

Because of this evolutionary advantage, you claim, the cobra carries the stone in a fleshy pocket in its head to prevent others of its species from seizing and monopolizing it. Thus *through accident and race memory*, you say, this behaviour is exhibited and the cobra learns to treasure this *precious natural decoy*.

My issue is with this last statement. I have studied snakes in the Punjab area of Pakistan. I have also travelled to the desert of Thal, looking for such 'naag manis' (for that is what the locals call the Cobra Stone), where nomadic tribesman claim to have seen giant snakes fighting over these pebbles. The only gems I found which emit green light are calcium fluorite crystals, which are easily fractured. However, Cobra Stones found by Berlin mineralogist Gustave Schubert in Mongolia's Tavan Bogd mountains are reported to have been so resistant to breakage that diamond-tipped tools cracked before their strength.

Gustave found these in a nest of *Ophiophagus hannah* – the King Cobra.

Which is why, I have concluded that none of the gems I found are Cobra Stones. Furthermore, I propose that none of the 'natural' fluorite crystals found near the habitat of the cobra are the mythical serpent stones. That the real Cobra Stone is a compound formed of cholorophane and unidentified biologically active substances in the glands of the *Ophiophagus hannah*; the snake might use for it for evolutionary or other advantages, but the process of its formation is entirely *within* the serpent's body, much as gallstones form in man and other species.

This conclusion is enthralling and in some ways wistful for me. The 'geo-natural' samples I recovered, which are breakable fluorite, have been deposited with the University of Punjab, and I am again in search of the real mythical stone. (You might be surprised to hear there are Indian and Pakistani herpetologists who have looked for it for decades. We are really a secret society!)

All flippancy aside, I have heard gossip among fellow seekers that the Panjnad area in southern Punjab (where all five Pakistani rivers come together) has an alluvial riverbed upon which sightings of these stones have occurred with astonishing frequency. Residents of a small desert town called Uch claim to have found and sold many such stones to tourists and local homeopaths. The report has piqued my interest, and I find myself wondering if I should make a visit to the area to further my studies.

Again, thank you for writing this gem of an article (you'll excuse the pun). It was a pleasure speculating on the possibilities such scenarios offer.

Sincerely,
Maliha Shafi, PhD
Associate Professor of Herpetology
University of Punjab, Pakistan

I raised my eyebrows.

'Still think I'm a fool for coming here?' Shafi said.

'She came to Uch in search of the Cobra Stone,' I said, piecing it all together. 'Probably with the qawwals, since they know the area. Why wouldn't she tell you before she left?'

'She used to do this kind of thing all the time. Go on these "research trips" without telling me. My Maliha was a wild one. You can take the girl out of the desert, I suppose, but you can't—' His gray eyes wandered, found the horizon, and settled on it. 'I thought she'd outgrow it, you know. I thought a day would come when she'd settle down. We would adopt children. We'd grow old together.' A salt-and-pepper stubble had grown on his cheeks. He rubbed it vigorously. 'May be something happened to her. God forbid, an accident perhaps. Otherwise, I know she would have returned home.'

I nodded. The letter seemed to be carefully worded. Maliha came across as thoughtful and practical. Imaginative, but calm and collected.

May be something *had* happened to her.

'Tell me more about this stone,' I said.

'Myth and speculation more than anything else. She was full of stories from her tribal days. She would laugh when she told them, watching my face as if she expected me to laugh at her.'

'Did you?' When he didn't reply, I asked, 'What stories?'

'Her favourite was the tale of the Serpent King and his queen. The Sheesh Naag, king of serpents, ruler of the underworld, asked his wife what she wanted for her hundredth name-day. The Serpent Queen, having grown tired of time's ravages upon her body, asked the king to grant her youth and everlasting beauty. The Sheesh Naag told her he couldn't reverse time, but he would grant her immortality via metamorphosis. By virtue of the stone's magic, she would turn into a beautiful woman, a snake-nymph with skin smooth and white as polished marble.

'The queen agreed. Since that day, on the lunar fourteenth when the moon is at it brightest, she rises from the underworld in human form and gazes upon our world, sighing at time's cruelty. Those who have seen her claim she wears the serpent pearl on her forehead.' Shafi tapped his own. 'It is said that this serpent stone is a gateway to other worlds than ours. That the possessor of the pearl shall rule animals and birds, be immune to all the venom in the world. Even become immortal.' Hakim shook his head. 'Oh, Maliha could tell these stories so dramatically.'

'It's dramatic all right.'

'Isn't it?' He smiled without mirth. 'And to think we're in the middle of it, travelling to find a woman who believes this gem really exists.'

'Her interest seems academic.'

'Like I said, my wife rationalized well. Want to guess which species of snake the Serpent King is according to legend?'

'Which?' When Shafi grinned, I knew. '*Ophiophagus hannah*,' I cried out. 'The King Cobra.'

He laughed, and for the first time in weeks it was open-throated and heartfelt. 'By Allah, that's it. Driver, what *is* it?'

The taxi driver had braked and stopped the car. Now he was getting out, muttering under his breath. 'Branches, sahib,' he said. 'Probably from a dust storm. They said one passed through here a few days back. I'll take care of them.'

We peered out. Two large branches lay across the road. Something large and white lay curled near them under a swarm of flies.

'What's that?' Shafi called.

A couple of vultures hopped back, hunching their shoulders as the driver approached, their yellow beady eyes fixed on him. 'Hussshhh,' yelled the taxi driver, waving his arms. 'Get out of here.' The vultures jerked their way to the gravel shoulder, where they waited. The driver called back: 'Roadkill, sahib.'

My gaze went to the blowflies, then to the carcass. Afternoon was dissolving into dusk, and I couldn't make out what it was. The driver lifted the second branch and heaved it at the vultures. They scattered, casting venomous looks at the intruder.

When the driver got back and turned the ignition, Shafi tapped him on the shoulder. 'What was it? Didn't look like a dog.'

'Nah, sahib.' The driver looked at us in the rearview mirror. 'A dead snake.'

Hakim looked at me, eyes wide, then laughed. I wouldn't

say anything. My heart thudded in my chest. Just beyond the tree line on our left stood a boy, arms crossed, hugging his chest. The woods were dark and, though he was too far for me to make out his features, I was sure it was the child I had seen at Hakim's clinic peering in through the window.

As I gripped the rolled down window, the boy turned and disappeared into the woods.

Indeed the qawwals are in town, and tonight they will sing, said the elderly owner of the guest house we were staying at.

A large musical mehfil was planned for the evening. Hundreds of people would gather at the shrine of Bibi Farida, a female mystic who died centuries ago. The qawwals would sing the nostalgic folklore of her life and the tireless work she did for Uch's children during a fatal dysentery epidemic.

'Who was she?' I asked.

The guest house owner shivered with reverence. 'An angel, sahib. Personification of Allah's mercy and glory,' he said in a voice garbled by toothlessness. 'Our elders used to say her goodness migrated into her skin. Her forehead shone with Allah's light. On dark nights, it could be seen for miles.'

'Who built the shrine?'

'An Irani prince who fell in love with her, they say. In the Mughal days Uch was a common route for Persian princes and emirs on their way to southern Indian cities. The prince wanted to marry her, but Bibi Farida declined, choosing her orphan paupers over the prince.'

It was our second day at the guest house, a small bungalow on the outskirts of Uch, situated on the banks of the River Panjnad. You could sit on the porch and drink tea and gaze into the night-darkened water.

Shafi had no interest in tea or scenic beauty. After two years of a relentless search, he was close to solving the mystery of his wife's disappearance, and the anticipation was gnawing at him. He rubbed his forehead, muttered prayers, and gripped his rosewood box – the one with the snake venom tin boxes – as if he'd never let go.

'Why'd you bring that?' I said.

His fingers drummed on the steel flip-lock. 'It was a present to her from my mother. Maliha used it for her trinkets before she went to University. The venoms are mine, but the box was always hers.'

'And what exactly do you plan to do with it?' A thought occurred to me. 'The venom you gave me for the shakes – does that have any lasting effects? Hallucinations etc?'

'No.' His eyebrows knotted. 'Why?'

'No reason,' I said, staring over his shoulders. The window was empty. I went to change into something comfortable.

At dusk we left on foot. Following our landlord's recommendation, we took the trail along the Panjnad River, a two-mile hike to the shrine.

The river breathed in and out, a shimmering tremulous line below the mud bank. In wind-hissing reeds and apluda grass rocks prostrated, like men crouched before a dark deity, their mineral-gleaming humps desolate. I thought of the floating bodies of my friends murdered by the Poison Men. Water birds cooed and flapped above us. The landscape of sand and mud sprawled into the water, and I saw a figure motionless in the distance, a dark speck haunting the liquid loneliness.

'No respite for the seeker,' murmured Shafi. I looked at him sharply, but he was staring at the ground, where mica and water-smoothed pebbles gleamed. The rosewood box rattled in his backpack with every step.

'Are you all right?'

He gave me a sunken-eyed smile. 'Never better.'

'What are we going to ask the qawwals? When we get there?'

He shrugged and shifted the backpack to the other shoulder. 'Whether a lady researcher came here with them.'

'What if they say no?'

'Then we ask others.' His smile was gone. 'Every fibre of my heart tells me she's here. Somewhere in this town.'

I held my tongue. What use disrupting any man's illusions? Hakim Shafi would leave no stone unturned in his search for his beloved, for it was clear to me that the man was maddened by love and had been for a long time. What kind of love, I didn't dare ponder. What does it take to raise a child bride – what transformative alchemy must happen between a man and a girl as age eats innocence and the infatuation evolves into its adult counterpart? I didn't want to think about it. The prospects were too disturbing.

We turned from the river to follow a winding trail leading up to Uch Lake, an artificial canal created by the dam at Panjnad head. That was where the shrine was located, the guest house owner had said.

'She once told me she loved snakes,' Shafi said, 'because when they shed their skins, they live anew. She said snakes are lovelier than butterflies, for a cocoon hides a butterfly's ugly childhood, while snakes don't bother about the artifice of beauty.'

We were nearing the shrine, and Shafi stopped. My heart lurched as we stood there, gazing at the structure towering before us.

'Holy heart of God,' Shafi said.

The shrine was spectacular, a dazzling three-tiered octagonal building erected on a sand base close to the lake. The top tier lifted the marble dome, while eight towers of carved timber supported the base tier. The exterior was patterned by many shades of blue and white mosaic tiles covered with coils of calligraphy in cyan and gold.

'The qawwals come here every year.' I gave a shuddering sigh. 'No wonder.'

It was a building of heartbreaking beauty, a glittering fortress in an arid landscape. It made me feel lonelier than ever. It made me want to flee from it.

Shafi's eyes glowed in a shaft of bleeding sunlight.

'Should we go in?' I said, gentle.

He nodded, his eyes fixed on the dome. Joining the throng of visitors, we passed under the arched gateway into the courtyard and crossed a sandy yard broken by rows of graves: sinners wanting the proximity of Bibi Farida.

The qawwals were gathered in front of the shrine proper, its entrance locked and bolted at this hour. A boisterous bunch, they chattered happily, their glances inevitably wandering back to their leader, a squat, obese, bald man, who waddled around the courtyard, greeting acquaintances with a wide smile under his handlebar mustache.

'That's him. Tariq Khan,' I whispered to Shafi. I nodded at the maestro as he passed by us. Shafi found us chairs five rows from the stage, and we sat.

'Do you want to talk to him now?'

Shafi scanned the crowd, his fingers trying in vain to find the phantom ends of the mustache he had shaved. 'After.'

The carpeted stage was adorned with four teakwood tablas, microphone pedestals, rolled silk pillows, and red-velveted bolster cushions. A harmonium fronted the tablas near a large tray filled with small paan-daans and filigreed spit utensils for the lead singer's betel-chewing and spitting pleasure.

Hakim leaned over. 'You see the harmonium?'

I glanced at it, then at him. 'Yes?'

'Look closer.'

I peered at it again. It was a beautiful hand-pumped

instrument crafted from rosewood, its white teeth gleaming in the spotlight. I could see nothing strange about it. 'What?'

Hakim reached out, took hold of my chin, and directed my gaze. 'Look at its right corner.'

I did.

Even from the fifth row, the white-and-gold symbol was visible against the dark mahogany: twin snakes coiled around a ruby emitting rays of light.

Sahib, my throat is dry. May I have some water?

Thank you for the shawl, sub-inspector sahib. The weather must be changing. Your station is so cold. I don't know how you get any work done. Although, I suppose, this chill is ideal for what you do here. More efficient to torture and break a freezing body.

Are they still out there, inspector sahib?

The Poison Men?

Come now, sahib, you can tell me. We both know I'm not leaving this station for a courtroom.

All right, sahib. As you wish.

About the music mehfil.

The shrine rang with the qawwals' music.

Dholki thumped, harmonium dueled with the vocal

alaap, and the background chorus clapped their hands to the tablas. The lead singer, a chubby, red-jowled man, screamed, his falsetto soaring high in the night.

Shafi was not impressed. 'I think my head's going to explode,' he whispered. 'Where *is* he?'

I shrugged. The maestro Tariq Khan hadn't made an appearance.

Shafi rose. 'I'm going to look for him,' he said, and disappeared between the aisles of chairs and bodies.

I laboured to my feet and combed the crowd: farmers, carpenters, shoemakers, shopkeepers. They swayed to the music. A strong earthy odour came from them, admixed with the sweet smell of cannabis. Some had bowls of bhang, which they downed like lassi. Mesmerized by the music, some had begun the *dhamaal*, the mystical dance in which the audience aspires to become the music. Eyes glazed, they jittered and whirled. A burly man, naked except for a dhoti, looked at me. A beatific smile on his face, he rolled up his sleeve and began to inject a pale liquid into his arm.

I turned away. It had been months since I touched the white queen, but the sight of that needle dimpling and piercing his skin left me shaky. My head pounded with the tabla beat. A woman laughed. Someone thrust a cup of bhang into my hand. Another clapped my back. I chugged the liquid. The crowd spun, the sky wheeled, and I glimpsed Hakim Shafi. He was slipping through a knot of turbaned labourers at the back of the crowd. I weaved my way after him, ignoring the mutterings in Saraiki and Punjabi. By the time I reached the labourers, Shafi was gone.

I don't know how long I was trapped in the crowd. Could have been minutes or hours. The migrainous music swelled and abated, the colours of the evening changed. Little pale children flitted between the legs of the surging audience.

At some point I stumbled from the grasping hands of the multitude to a narrow, uneven gravel path twisting through the shrine's outer towers. The night deepened and shadows swivelled, pirouetting to the drumbeat, and I found myself in front of an arched postern door.

A padlock hung open from the latch like a broken jaw. I gazed at it. The keyhole stirred. A threadlike black snake nosed its head out, slithered down the door and disappeared into the gravel. I pushed the door open. Beyond was a black gullet softened by gleams of distant green light.

I went in.

The corridor came at me with drunken angles – perhaps I was drunk with the bhang from the mehfil. The qawwali music receded and was replaced by an unnerving quiet. Benighted by the meanderings of the corridor, I lurched into walls and cave mouths that reared open before me.

A burst of light drew me out into a vast space. I slitted my eyes against its acid-green shine. The uneven stone floor, the dip and rise of the ceiling, the damp feel of granite beneath my fingers – this was a natural chamber of some sort. A cavern under the shrine.

The light was a pulsing verdant web, retreating and expanding with my breath. Something moved in the web's centre. I raised a hand and plunged forward. The light source materialized: it was the top of a large marble slab. A gravestone.

Hakim Shafi stood over it, his back to me.

His shirt was torn. The rosewood box lay discarded at his feet. He might have been a scarecrow's relief in the green light, except that the portly maestro Tariq Khan leaned and whispered in his ears.

I froze, my feet magnetized to the stone floor. The maestro didn't turn to look at me. His thick lips puckered like fat slugs near Shafi's earlobes, his chubby fingers gripping Shafi's wrist. A humming sound came from him. I strained to listen and discovered that he was singing.

Sahib, I swear on my mother's grave, I have not been more horrified or enthralled in my life. The paunchy qawwal's stomach heaved as he whisper-sang into Hakim Shafi's ears. Strange melodies slithered across the thrashing web of light. A gurgling song made from vowels, a deep vibrato alaap that lunged and pitched, as if the maestro intended to gut the cavern walls.

I readied myself to ram and shove Tariq Khan's massive bulk off my friend. But the maestro dropped Shafi's wrist and withdrew his lips from Shafi's ears.

The hakim shuddered and let out a sigh.

The maestro threw his head back and began to sing at the ceiling.

Emerald light blazed. The gravestone shook and the light source shook with it, throwing shadows of the two men across the ground, stretching them like tar. Shafi jerked, as if in the throes of a seizure, and turned around, smacking his lips. His eyes shone like moonstones. 'My darling,' I thought he said; in the wails from Tariq Khan I couldn't be sure. The maestro sang and stepped back, sang and back-trotted, until he stood at the far end of the cavern, his inhuman music lapping across the stony distance. It turned my blood viscous.

Something shimmered at Shafi's feet. A child. No, a woman crouching, with hair like moonbeams. She rose and Shafi gazed at her with awe, at the clearness of her skin, the perfection of her nose, her moving lips. She plucked the glowing stone from the grave slab and affixed it to her forehead, where it shone, the brightest star there ever was. She drew herself tall and smiled. Shafi grinned back. She whispered. The sound was like insects rubbing their legs together, or lonely reeds sighing on cold alien shores, or hundreds of serpents—

'You could have just asked me to join you. Why make me suffer?' Shafi said, and laughed at the intensified buzzing that came from her. Did he think she was his wife? In the throbbing light, the woman's features blurred, softened, became a child's, and for a moment they were so terribly familiar that sweat broke out on my forehead.

With the slightest steps I retreated into the dark. The woman's hissing came loud and suddenly lucid. Words were buried in its ancient cadence – a monstrous lullaby or a *self-*annihilating qawwali.

Tariq Khan was gone. Sometime between the woman's apparition and her whispering, the maestro's song had stopped. The cavern was quiet, except for her murmurs. Her bone-white hands settled on Shafi's shoulders, drawing him close, and she was now taller than he.

'Anything for you, my love,' Shafi was saying, even as she lowered her face to his, her skin glistening in the light. Drool fell from the corner of her mouth, snaked down Shafi's cheeks, inflaming them. He grinned wider and licked his lips. 'Anything.'

She wrapped herself around him, arms then legs lifting and coiling. Her weight staggered him for a moment, but he recovered and stood swaying as she hung from him, a giant spider or a leech planted on his flesh. Her eyes burned, her lips never stopped moving. The light cascaded around their conjoined bodies, and I thought of giant cobras in sprawling fields playing with fireflies.

I must have cried out, for she raised her head and gazed at me. Her eyes were green, like squeezed summer grass. Like strange planets roaming across a vast black cosmos reflecting light from dying suns. Like the jade-coloured dress a king might have gifted his queen, come another spring.

Dreamily she smiled at me, this marble-skinned woman, showing her fangs, and the terror in my heart was great. Deranged thoughts raced through my mind: this is the queen the true white queen and up till now whatever we imagined about the world, our world, their world was a mote of dust licking its own tail in the tiniest sliver of light unaware of the dark wrought endless around it.

She jerked her head away. The spell broke. I wobbled and fell to the floor and hugged my chest. The Lady of the Stone kissed Shafi's neck. Her lips parted and sharp teeth, like nails from a nail gun, drove into his flesh.

Shafi closed his eyes, sighed, and began to pant.

He never stopped panting.

Even as the venom softened him and melted his face. Shafi's flesh gurgled and fell away. Her legs fused at his back and her skin began to shed, revealing a diamond-patterned second skin. Her fingernails tore at Shafi, flayed him, unhooking his flesh from its burdensome wrapping, and the toxin congealed his blood and plugged the gashes. Her teeth and fingers roved and split, peeled and stretched, so when she was done Hakim Shafi was a pillar of clotted blood and watery bone pulsating with the beat of his encased heart.

The snakewoman paused, examined her handiwork, angled her head, and opened her jaws. Wide, wider, stretch, expand, until her maw was a black gullet around which flared her spectacled, ribbed hood. Her mouth crackled and thrust and wrapped around Shafi's bubbling head. His eyelids were gone, his pupils dull, and I saw he was still trying to smile.

Sahib, I… I cannot go on.

I need to breathe. I cannot breathe.

Inspector sahib, you sit there, smug.

You're thinking to yourself that you've proven beyond doubt that this junkie, this peddler, this heroinchi, is mad. I am a raving lunatic who murdered Hakim Shafi and secreted his body someplace so you couldn't find it. You say to yourself, a little more, just a little more nonsense out of him for the Poison Men, and you can wrap it all up and call it a night. Cold iron bars for the maniac with vermin for company, and a warm bed for you and the sub-inspector, with your wives pressing your sore legs before you sleep.

You are wrong, sahib. Just like I was.

I know this now. Our world is not our own, it is borrowed. Sometimes it may be shared, occasionally even reshaped against the will of its possessors, but always for a brief interlude.

We heroinchies are neither lovers nor children of the white queen. The children of the true white queen lurk in shadow and live in rumour. A secret whispered from midnight doorways. A species seamed into the skin of our puny civilization, they crawl forth only at the call of their mistress.

Which is why I did what I did, and why I didn't flee when they showed themselves. As the white queen's spawn surged from the cavern's depths that night, a tide of venomous children washing over the smoking blood column that was once Hakim Shafi, it came together in my head. At last I understood why I had been saved the night I died in the park.

The snakewoman's translucent children licked and gorged on the lower half of Hakim Shafi; he was already waist-deep inside their mother's maw. As his blood steamed, they chased the red smoke with their spade-shaped muzzles. They followed the vapours with their snouts and lapped the condensate. Their smacking, slurping sounds echoed in the green-lit cave long after they'd dragged Shafi away, their mother still riding his head.

It took all my will to creep forward and seize the rosewood box. It was slick with slime. When I turned I nearly fell across the snakeskin molted on the floor – yards of a squamous, leathery thing that twitched like a lizard's tail.

I reached out with a shaky hand. In the secret light of the cavern, the snakeskin blossomed and inscriptions emerged: geometric patterns, jagged whorls and spiraling curlicues. An enchanted map borne of the white queen's flesh. A primeval cosmos unfurled like a lotus dipped in blood. How the light made its mysteries glow! They burned into my eyes so everywhere I looked the universe was naked and serpentine, the light of the snake pearl limning its secrets – and when I looked down, I saw particles of my own skin shedding as I became something new and irresolute.

I gasped at the enchantment. The light twitched and

the snakewoman's hum wrapped around me. Love me, it said. Stay with me. I shall show you sights handsome and teach you ways of embracing your astonishment. Worship me and you shall neither want nor dream nor fear again. Not even your little boy.

Then there were too many faces in the cavern. They dripped from the ceiling, they draped the floor, they licked with blackened tongues the soughed membrane of their mother. I dropped the snakeskin and they swarmed around me, pale and leering.

I screamed. Clutching the rosewood box, I whirled and ran. Back the way I came, up the dark corridor leading into this den of quietus, the domain of the Lady of the Stone with her green gem shining like a murderous beacon.

Before I bolted into the tunnel, I turned for a last look and saw what I thought was a cave was really an ossuary. The walls were lined with skulls and bones, and the wetness of the granite was moss flourishing on snakeskins tautened across this ossified legion.

A yellow moon sickled the night clouds when I stumbled out the postern door on to the brick path that wound through the shrine's towers. Somewhere a cock crowed.

The qawwals and their audience were gone. Brass bowls and bottles, used needles, and crushed joints lay scattered on the ground. I staggered past graves filled with glorified sinners. My stomach heaved. I think at one point I vomited on a grave, yanking at cemetery dandelions to wipe my mouth. Then I laboured on, the rosewood box under my arm, until my lungs were on fire, and I collapsed on the banks of Uch Lake.

I might have lain there for hours. I dozed and dreamed, and in my dreams the lake and the river and all the blue waters of the world were nothing but one colossal snake wrapped around the earth. The moon and the sun were its alien eyes, the horizon the burning flare of its hood upholding the heavens.

I thought of Tariq Khan and his band of qawwals and the town of Uch and the townsfolk. I thought of the little pale children I had seen at Hakim Shafi's clinic and on my journey into the queen's realm. Who watched Shafi? Who watched us all? Curled I lay and dreamed foetal dreams; and at some point I awoke and went to the lake and drank. I opened the rosewood box and from it I took Shafi's venoms, mixed the powders, and tossed fistfuls into the water. Coppery-red and black drifted in the wind, blew in veils across the lake's surface, and I thought again of Shafi's steaming offal billowing from the pillar of his petrified blood.

When the tins were empty, I looked inside the box and saw the sandstone necklace Shafi's wife had left behind. I flung it into the lake then went back to the guest house, where I gathered Shafi's things, called a taxi, and left the wretched town of Uch. I had enough money to be taken to Sangchoor, a nearby town, and there, in a shabby motel, I hid and waited.

Two days later, news came that a hundred people, including a band of qawwals, had sickened from a mysterious epidemic in Uch. Five days later, the papers said, traces of potent poisons were found in the blood of some who died. Foul play was suspected.

Seven days later, the tribe of the white queen came for me.

A river of faces flowed in the walls of my motel room. I glimpsed them in the ceiling cracks, heard their chatter in the eaves, felt them thump against the windowpane. One night the torrent rushed at the glass, hit and broke into a million poisonous children – tiny-limbed, gelid and familiar. They exhaled fog on the glass. They wore gaping expressions that dissolved and reemerged. Last night, they came for me again, and...and sahib, I was done. I was utterly exhausted.

Which was why, I decided to come to your police station.

This is my story, sahib. Of a heroinchi courting a third death.

I see by your eyes that you don't know which part to believe. That I am mad and tried to murder a hundred people, many of them children, or that under the shrine of Bibi Farida, there breathes a different life. The paradox of my insanity doesn't nullify either truth.

I am cold, sahib. So cold. Just look at my arms – have you ever seen such hideous discolouration, such scales? I know what Hakim Shafi would say: I touched his poisons with my bare hands, but that's not it. Already I can feel my fingers shrivelling, the skin becoming thick and cracked above the knuckles. I have difficulty chewing, as if my jaws have become too big for my meals. My teeth are so pointed they seem suited for a different purpose now. I would go to a doctor, but which antidote would they give me? I handled hundreds of those poisons, I handled *her* skin, and...well, only like can heal like.

What is it they say about God? He was a hidden treasure who created us to discover himself. May be goddesses do that too. Especially goddesses longing to return to their people.

I see your eyes. You think I killed them both, Shafi and her.

You're standing up. Of course. You have to hand me over to the Poison Men. I do wonder how they found me this quickly. Perhaps a phone call from you? But how did *you* know I was wanted? How did the police inspector of Sangchoor know gangland members from the big cities wanted me?

I wonder why their shadows look bloated and misshaped when they pass the window. Why, they seem to be holding a *drum* under their arms. It almost looks like a tabla.

It's so difficult to keep everything in order in my head. I keep returning to the song the Serpent Queen sang. It warbles in my head, it whips my bones. Perhaps I shall hear it when they slice my throat. Her words – they come to me in my dreams, buried in that hissing cacophony. Magic words, ancient words, shards of glass in an ambrosial meal:

'I live in your soul's crevices. I have lived forever there.
Like a moth to dancing light you'll come; while I still prepare
to skewer you with my arrow, to noose my hair locks flung.
I'll whip out my tresses, grin and show:
dead lovers on each blade hung.'

THE VAPORIZATION ENTHALPY OF A PECULIAR PAKISTANI FAMILY

1

The Solid Phase of Matter is a state wherein a substance is particulately bound. To transform a solid into liquid, the intermolecular forces need to be overcome, which may be achieved by adding energy. The energy necessary to break such bonds is, ironically, called the *heat of fusion*.

On a Friday after juma prayers, under the sturdy old oak in their yard, they came together as a family for the last time. Her brother gave in and wept as Tara watched, eyes prickling with warmth that wouldn't disperse no matter how much she knuckled them.

'Monsters,' Sohail said. He wiped his mouth with the back of his hand and looked at the sky, a vast blue cobblestoned with heat. The wheat fields beyond the steppe on which their house perched were baked and khaki and shivered a little under Tara's feet. An earthquake or a vehicle passing on the highway? Perhaps it was just foreknowledge that made her dizzy. She pulled at her lower lip.

'Monsters,' Sohail said again, voice raspy. 'Oh God, Apee. Murderers.'

She touched his shoulders. 'I'm sorry.' She thought he would pull back. When he didn't, she let her fingers fall and linger on the flame-shaped scar on his arm. So it begins, she thought. How many times has this happened before? Pushing and prodding a people ceaselessly, until night swallows us whole. She thought of that until her heart constricted with dread. 'Don't do it,' she said. 'Don't go.'

Sohail lifted his shoulders and drew his head back, watched her as if seeing her for the first time.

'I know I ask too much,' she said. 'I know the customs of honour, but for the love of God let it go. One death needn't become a lodestone for others. One horror needn't—'

But he wasn't listening, she could tell. They would neither hear nor see once the blood was upon them; didn't the scriptures say so? Sohail heard, but didn't listen. His conjoined eyebrows, like dark hands held, twitched. 'Her name meant a rose,' he said and smiled. It was heartbreakingly beautiful, his smile, frightening. 'Under the mango trees by Chacha Barkat's farm Gulminay told me that as I kissed her hand. Whispered it in my ear, her finger circling my temple. *A rose blooming in the rain.* Did you know that?'

Tara didn't. 'Yes,' she said, looking into eyes that were webbed with red, thin tendrils of steam rising from them. The sorrow of his confession filled her now, as did the certainty of his leaving. 'A rose God gave us and took away because He loved her so.'

'Wasn't God,' Sohail said. He turned his back to her and was able to speak rapidly, 'I leave tomorrow at dawn. I shall take some bread and meat and go to the mountains. I will stay there until I'm shown a sign, and once I am...' His back arched then straightened. He had lost weight; his shoulder blades poked through the khaddar shirt like trowels. 'I will arise and go to their homes. I will go to them as God's wrath. I—'

She cut him off. 'What if you go to them and die? What if you go to them a steer to the slaughter? And Ma and I – what if months later we sit here and watch a dusty vehicle climb the hill, bouncing a sack of meat in the back that was once you? What if...'

But she couldn't keep giving name to her terrors. Instead, she said, 'If you go, know that we as we are now will be forever gone.'

'*We* were gone when *she* was gone. We were shattered with her bones.' The wind picked up, a whipping, chador-lifting gust that made Tara's flesh prickle. Sohail began to walk down the steppes, each with its own crop: tobacco, corn, rice wavering in knee-high water; and as she watched his lean farmer body move away, it seemed to her as if his back was drenched not in sweat, but acid. That his flesh glistened not from moisture, but blood. All at once their world was just too much, or not enough – Tara couldn't decide which – and the weight of the future pressed on her until she couldn't breathe. 'My brother,' she said and her voice shook. 'You're my little brother.'

Sohail continued walking his careful, dead man's walk until his head was a wobbling black pumpkin rising from the last steppe. She watched him disappear into the undulations of her motherland, unable to stop the irrevocable fracturing of her world, wondering if he would doubt, stop and look back.

Sohail didn't look back.

Ma died three months later.

The village menfolk told her the death prayer was brief but moving. Tara couldn't attend because she was a woman.

They helped her bury Ma's sorrow-filled body, and the rotund mullah clucked and murmured over the fresh mound. The women hugged her and crooned and urged her to vent. 'Weep, our daughter,' they cried, 'for children's tears borne of love are manna for the departed parent.'

Tara tried to weep and felt guilty when she couldn't. Ma had been sick and in pain for a long time and her death was a mercy, but you couldn't say that. Besides, the women had said *children*, and Sohail wasn't there. Not at the funeral, not in the days after. Tara dared not imagine his beautiful face gleaming in the dark atop a stony mountain, persevering in his vigil.

'What will you do now?' they asked, gathering around her with sharp, interested eyes. She knew what they really meant. A young widow with no family was a stranger amidst her clan. At best an oddity, at worst a seductress. Tara was surprised when their concern didn't frighten her. The perfect estrangement of it, the inadmissible exclusion – they were just more beads in the tautening string of her life.

'I'm thinking of going to the City,' she told them. 'Ma has a cousin there. Perhaps he can help me with bread and board, while I look for work.'

She paused, startled by a clear memory: Sohail and Gulminay by the Kunhar River, fishing for trout. Gulminay's sequined hijab dappling the stream with emerald as she reached into the water with long, pale fingers. Sohail with his stupid lover's grin, his hands encircling her waist – and Tara watching them both from the shade of the eucalyptus, affectionate and jealous. By then Tara's husband was long gone and she could forgive herself the occasional resentment.

'Yes, I think I might go to the city for a while,' Tara said and laughed. The sound rang strange in the emptiness of her tin-and-timber house. 'Who knows I might even go back to school. I used to enjoy studying once.' She smiled at these women with their sympathetic, hateful eyes that watched her as they would a rabid animal. She nodded, talking mostly to herself. 'Yes, that would be good. Hashim would've wanted that.'

They drew back from her, from her late husband's mention. Why not? Everything she touched fell apart; everyone around her died or went missing. There was no judgment here, just dread-filled awe. She could allow them that, she thought.

2

The Liquid Phase of Matter is a restless volume that, by dint of the vast spaces between its molecules, fills any container it is poured in and takes its shape. Liquids tend to have higher energy than solids, and while the particles retain inter-particle forces they have enough energy to move relative to each other.

The structure therefore becomes mobile and malleable.

In the City Tara turned feral in her pursuit of learning. This was long coming. At 13 she had been withdrawn from school; she needed not homework but a husband, she was told. At 16 she was wedded to Hashim; he was blown to smithereens on her 21st birthday. A suicide attack on his unit's northern check post.

'I want to go to school,' she told Wasif Khan, her mother's cousin. They were sitting in his yard, peeling fresh oranges he had confiscated from an illegal food vendor. Wasif was a police hawaldar and on the rough side of 60. He often said confiscation was his first love and contraband second. He grinned when he said it, which made it easier for her to like him.

Now Wasif tossed a half-gnawed chicken bone to his mongrel and said, 'I don't know if you want to do that.'

'I do.'

'You need a husband, not—'

'I don't care. I need to go back to school.'

'Why?' He dropped an orange rind in the basket at his feet, gestured with a liver-spotted hand. 'The City doesn't care if you can read. Besides, I need someone to help me around the house. I'm old and ugly and useless, but I have this tolerable place and no children. You're my cousin's daughter. You can stay here for as long as you like.'

In a different time she might have mistaken his generosity for loneliness, but now she took it for what it was. Such was the way of age: it melted prejudice or hardened it. 'I want to learn about the world,' she said. 'I want to see if there are others like me. If there have been others before me.'

He was confused. 'Like you how?'

She rubbed an orange peel between her fingers, pressing the fibrous texture of it in the creases of her flesh, considering how much to tell him. Her mother had trusted him. Yet Ma hardly had their gift and even if she did Tara doubted she would have been open about it. Ma had been wary of giving too much of herself away, a trait she passed on to both her children. Among other things.

So now Tara said, 'Others who *need* to learn more about themselves. I spent my adolescence being a wife and look where that got me. I am left with nothing. No children, no husband, no family.' Wasif Khan looked hurt. She smiled kindly. 'You know what I mean, Uncle. I love you, but I need to love me too.'

Wasif Khan tilted his head back and pinched a slice of orange above his mouth. Squeezed it until his tongue and remaining teeth gleamed with the juice. He closed his eyes and sighed. 'I don't know if I approve, but I think I understand. It's a different time. Others my age who don't realize it don't fare well. Traditional rules don't apply any more, you know. Sometimes, I think that is wonderful. Other times, it feels like the whole damn world is conspiring against you.'

She rose, picking up her mess and his. 'Thank you for letting me stay here.'

'It's either you or every hookah-sucking asshole in this neighbourhood for company.' He grinned and shrugged his shoulders. 'My apologies. I've been living alone too long and my tongue is spoilt.'

She laughed loudly, and thought of a blazing cliff somewhere from which dangled two browned, peeling, inflamed legs, swinging back and forth like pendulums.

She read everything she could get her hands on. At first, her letters were broken and awkward, like her rusty brain, but she did it anyway. It took her two years, but eventually she qualified to sit for FA exams and passed.

'I don't know how you did it,' Wasif Khan told her, his face beaming as he handed out sweetmeats to neighbourhood children, 'but I'm proud of you.'

She didn't know what she felt. Once the children left, she went to the mirror and gazed at her reflection, flexing her arm this way and that, making the flame-shaped scar bulge. We all drink the blood of yesterday, she thought.

The next day she enrolled in Punjab University's BSc programme.

In biology, they learned about plants and animals. Flora and fauna, they called them. Things constructed piece by piece from the basic units of life – cells. These cells in turn were made from tiny building blocks called atoms, which themselves were bonded by the very things that repelled their core: electrons.

In physics, she learned what electrons were. Little flickering ghosts that vanished and reappeared as they pleased. Her flesh was empty, she discovered, or most of it. So were human bones and solid buildings and the incessantly agitated world and the universe. All that immense loneliness and darkness, with only a hint that we existed. The idea awed her. Did we exist only as a possibility?

In Wasif Khan's yard was a tall mulberry tree. On her way to school she touched its saw-like leaves; they were spiny and jagged. She hadn't had mulberries in a while. She picked a basketful, nipped her wrist with her teeth and let her blood roast a few. She watched them smoke and curl from the heat of her genes, inhaled the sweet steam of their juice as they turned into mystical symbols.

Mama would have been proud.

She ate them with salt and pepper and was offended when Wasif Khan wouldn't touch the remaining.

He said they gave him reflux.

3

The Gaseous Phase of Matter is one in which particles have enough kinetic energy to render intermolecular forces negligible. A gas, therefore, will occupy the entire container in which it is confined.

Liquid may be converted to gas by heating at constant pressure to a certain temperature.

This temperature is called the *boiling point*.

The worst flooding in 40 years was the one thing all radio broadcasters agreed on.

Wasif Khan hadn't confiscated a television yet, but if he had, Tara knew it would just confirm the cataclysmic damage the radio was reporting. At one point, someone said, an area the size of England was submerged in floodwater.

Their neighbourhood in the City's periphery escaped the worst devastation, but Tara and Wasif witnessed it daily when they went for rescue work: upchucked power pylons and splintered oak trees smashed through vending stalls in the market; murderous tin and steel sheets slicing through inundated alleys; bloated dead cows and sheep eddying in shoulder-high water with terrified children clinging to them. It pawed at towering steel-and-concrete structures, this liquid death that had come to the city; it ripped out their underpinnings and annihilated everything in its path.

Tara survived these days of heartbreak and horror by helping set up a small tent city on the sports fields of her university. She volunteered to establish a nursery for displaced children and went with rescue teams to scour the ruins for usable supplies and corpses.

As she pulled out the dead and living from beneath the wreckage, as she tossed food rations and clothes to the dull-eyed homeless, she thought of how bright and hot and dry the spines of her brother's mountains must be. It had been four years since she saw him, but her dreams were filled with his absence. Did he sit parched and caved in, like a deliberate Buddha? Or was he dead and pecked on by ravens and falcons?

She shuddered at the thought and grabbed another packet of cooked rice and dry beans for the benighted survivors.

The first warning came on the last night of Ramadan. Chand raat.

Tara was eating bread and lentils with her foundling children in the nursery when it happened. A bone-deep tremble that ran through the grass, flattening its blades, evaporating the evening dew from them. Seconds later, a distant boom followed: a hollow rumble that hurt Tara's ears and made her feel nauseated. (Later, she would learn the blast had torn through the marble-walled shrine of Data Sahib, wrenching its iron fence from its moorings, sending jagged pieces of metal and scorched human limbs spinning across the walled part of the City.)

Her children sat up, confused and scared. Tara soothed them. Once a replacement was found, she went to talk to the tent city administrator.

'I've seen this before,' she told him once he confirmed it was a suicide blast. 'My husband and sister-in-law died in similar circumstances. Usually an attack like this is followed by another when rescue attempts are made. My husband used to call them "double tap" attacks.' She paused, thinking of his kind face for the first time in months. 'He understood the barbaric reasoning behind them.'

The administrator, a chubby, short man, scratched his chin. 'How come?'

'He was in Frontier Corps. He tackled such situations before he was killed.'

'Condolences, bibi.' The administrator's face crinkled with sympathy. 'But what does that have to do with us?'

'Sometimes terrorists will use the first attack like a decoy and go after other civilian structures.'

'Thank you for the warning. I'll send out word to form a volunteer perimeter patrol.' He scrutinized her, taking in her hijab, the bruised elbows and grimy fingernails from days of work. 'God bless you for the lives you've already saved. And for all your hard work.'

He handed her a packet of boiled corn and alphabet books. She nodded, the carnage from the shrine vivid inside her head, thanked him and left.

An emergency broadcast 30 minutes later confirmed her fear: a second blast at Data Sahib blew up a fire engine, obliterated a jeep filled with policemen and vapourized 25 rescuers. Five of these were female medical students. Their glass bangles were melted and their headscarves burned to cinders by the time the Emergency Medical Service came.

Tara didn't weep when she heard. In her heart was a steaming shadow that whispered nasty things. It impaled her with its familiarity, and a dreadful suspicion grew in her that the beast was rage and wore a face she knew well.

4

When matter is heated to high temperatures, such as over a flame, electrons begin to leave the atoms. At very high temperatures, essentially all electrons are assumed to be dissociated, resulting in a unique state wherein positively charged nuclei swim in a raging 'sea' of free electrons.

This state is called the Plasma Phase of Matter and exists in lightning, electric sparks, neon lights and the Sun.

In a rash of terror attacks, the City came apart: the Tower of Pakistan, Lahore Fort, Iqbal's Memorial, Shalimar Gardens, Anarkali's Tomb, all the gates of the Walled City. They exploded and fell in burning tatters, survived only by a quivering bloodhaze through which peeked the haunted eyes of their ghosts.

This is death, this is love, this is the comeuppance of the two, as the world according to you will finally come to an end. So snarled the beast in Tara's head each night. The tragedy of the floodwaters was not over yet, and now this.

Tara survived this new world through her books and her children. The two seemed to have become one: pages filled with loss. White space itching to be written, reshaped, incinerated. Sometimes, she would bite her lip and let the trickle of blood stain her fingers, touch them to paper, watch it catch fire and flutter in the air, like a phoenix. A glamour created by tribulation. Then again, we were all glamours, weren't we? Tara reminded herself of the beautiful emptiness of it all, even as the City and her tears burned, and she forced herself to smile.

Until one morning when she awoke and discovered that, in the cover of the night, a suicide bomber had hit her tent city's perimeter patrol.

After the others left, she stood over her friends' graves in the twilight.

Overhead kites and vultures unzipped the darkness in circles. Tara remembered how cold it was when they lowered Gulminay's remains in the ground. How the drone attack had torn her limbs clean off so a glistening, misshapen, idiot torso remained below a shrivelled head. She remembered Ma, too, and how she was killed by her son's love. The first of many murders.

'I know you,' she whispered to the Beast resident in her soul. 'I know you', and all the time she scribbled on her flesh with a glass shard she found buried in a patrolman's eye. Her wrist glowed with her heat and that of her ancestors. She watched her blood bubble and surge skyward. To join the plasma of the world and drift its soft, vaporous way across the darkened City; and she wondered again if she was still capable of loving them both.

The administrator promised her he would take care of her children. He gave her food and a bundle of long shirts and shalwars. He asked her where she was going, and she knew he was afraid for her.

'I will be all right,' she told him. 'I know someone who lives up there.'

'I don't understand why you must go. It's dangerous,' he said, his flesh red under the hollows of his eyes. He wiped his cheeks. 'I wish you didn't have to. But I suppose you will. I see that in your face. I saw that when you first came here.'

She laughed. The sound of her laughter saddened her. 'The world will change,' she said. 'It always does. We are all empty, but this changing is what saves us. That is why I must go.'

He nodded. She smiled. They touched hands briefly; she stepped forward and hugged him, her headscarf tickling his nostrils, making him sneeze. She giggled and told him how much she loved him and the others. He looked pleased, and she saw how much kindness and gentleness lived inside his skin, how his blood would never boil with undesired heat.

She lifted his finger, kissed it, wondering at how solid his vacant flesh felt against her lips.

Then she turned and left him, leaving water and fire and the crackling, hissing earth of the City behind.

Such was how Tara Khan left for the mountains.

The journey took a week. The roads were barren, the landscape abraded by floodwater, flensed by intermittent fires. Shocked trees, stripped of fruit, stood rigid and receding as Tara's bus rolled by, their gnarled limbs pointing accusatorially at the heavens.

Wrapped in her chador, headscarf and khaddar shalwar kameez, Tara folded into the rugged barrenness with its rugged people. They were not unkind; even in the midst of madness, they held on to their traditions of honour and hospitality, allowing Tara to scout for hints of the Beast's presence. The northerners chattered constantly. They were horrified by the atrocities they saw on TV and the ones she reported, and because she spoke Pashto they treated her like one of them.

Tara kept her ears open. Rumours, whispers, beckonings by skeletal fingers. Someone said there was a man in Abbottabad who was the puppeteer. Another shook his head and said that was a shadow show put up by the perpetrators. That the Supreme Conspirator was swallowed by earth soaked with the blood of thousands and lived only as an extension of this irredeemable evil.

Tara listened and tried to read between their words. Slowly, the hints in the midnight alleys, the leprous grins, grasping fingers, incinerated trees and smoldering skulls began to come together and form a map.

Tara followed it into the heart of the mountains.

5

When the elementary particle boson is cooled to temperatures near absolute zero, a dilute 'gas' is created. Under such conditions, a large number of bosons occupy the lowest quantum state and an unusual thing happens: quantum effects become visible on a macroscopic scale. This effect is called the macroscopic quantum phenomena and the 'Bose–Einstein condensate' is inferred to be a new state of matter. The presence of one such particle, the Higgs–Boson, was tentatively confirmed on 14 March

2013 in the most complex experimental facility built in human history.

This particle is sometimes called the *God Particle*.

When she found him, he had changed his name.

There is a story told around campfires since the beginning of time: Millennia ago a stone fell from the infinity of space and plunked on to a statistically impossible planet. The stone was round, smaller than a marble, and carried a word inscribed on it.

It has been passed down generations of Pahari clans that that word is the *Ism-e-Azam*, the Most High Name of God.

Every sect in the history of our world has written about it. Egyptians, Mayans, Jewish, Christian and Muslim mystics. Some have described it as the primal point from which existence began, and that the Universal Essence lives in this *nuktah*.

The closest inheritor to the First Word, some say, is one who originated in Mesopotamia, the land between two rivers. The Sumerians called him *Annunaki*.

He of Godly Blood.

Tara thought of this oral tradition and sat down at the mouth of the demolished cave. She knew he lived inside, for everything near the cave mouth reeked of his heat. Twisted boulders stretched granite hands toward it like pilgrims at the Kaaba. The heat of the stars they both carried in their genes, in the sputtering, whisking emptiness of their cells, had leached out and warped the mountains and the path leading up to it.

Tara sat cross-legged in the lotus position her mother taught them when they were young. She took a sharp rock and ran it across her palm. Crimson droplets appeared and evaporated, leaving a metallic tang in the air. She sat and inhaled that smell and thought of the home that once was. She thought of her mother and her husband; of Gulminay and Sohail; of the floods (Did he have something to do with that too? Did his rage liquefy snow-topped mountains and drown an entire country?); of suicide bombers and the university patrol; of countless human eyes that flicked each moment to an unforgiving sky, where mercy may or may not live; and her eyes began to burn and at last Tara Khan began to cry.

'Come out,' she said between her sobs. 'Come out, Beast. Come out, Rage. Come out, Death of the Two Worlds and all that lives in between. Come out, Monster. Come out, Fear', and all the while she rubbed her eyes and let the salt of her tears crumble between her fingertips. She looked at the white crystals, flattened them, and screamed, 'Come out, ANNUNAKI.'

And in a belch of shrieking air and a blast of heat her brother came to her.

They faced each other.

His skin was gone. His eyes melted, his nose bridge collapsed; the bones underneath were simmering white seas that rolled and twinkled across the constantly melting and rearranging meat of him. His limbs were pseudopodic, his movement that of a softly turning planet drifting across the possibility that is being.

Now he floated to her on a gliding plane of his skin. His potent heat, a shifting locus of time-space with infinite energy roiling inside it, touched her, making her recoil. When he breathed, she saw everything that once was and knew what she knew.

'Salam,' she said. 'Peace be upon you, brother.'

The *nuktah* that was him twitched. His fried vocal cords were not capable of producing words any more.

'I used to think,' she continued, watching the infinitesimal shifting of matter and emptiness inside him, 'that love was all that mattered. That the bonds that pull us all together are of timeless love. But it is not true, is it? It has never been true.'

He shimmered, and said nothing.

'I still believe, though. In existing. In *ex nihilo nihil fit*. If nothing comes from nothing, we cannot return to it. Ergo, life has a reason and needs to *be*.' She paused, remembering a day when her brother plucked a sunflower from a lush meadow and slipped it into Gulminay's hair. 'Gulminay-jaan once was and still is. Perhaps inside me and you.' Tara wiped her tears and smiled. 'Even if most of us is nothing.'

The heat-thing that was her brother slipped forward a notch. Tara rose to her feet and began walking towards it. The blood in her vasculature seethed and raged.

'Even if death breaks some bonds and forms others. Even if the world quivers, implodes, and becomes a grain of sand.'

Annunaki watched her through eyes like black holes and gently swirled.

'Even if we have killed and shall kill. Even if the source is nothing if not grief. Even if sorrow is the distillate of our life.'

She reached out and gripped his melting amoebic limb. He shrank, but didn't let go, as the maddened heat of her essence surged forth to meet his.

'Even if we don't amount to much. Even if the sea of our consciousness breaks against the shore of quantum impossibilities.'

She pressed his now-arm, her fingers elongating, stretching, turning, fusing; her flame-scar rippled and coiled to probe for his like a proboscis.

Sohail tried to smile. In his smile were heat-deaths of countless worlds, supernova bursts and the chrysalis sheen of a freshly hatched larva. She thought he might have whispered *sorry*. That in another time and universe there were not countless intemperate blood-children of his spreading across the earth's face like vitriolic tides rising to obliterate the planet. That all this was not really happening for one misdirected missile, one careless press of a button by a soldier eating junk food and licking his fingers.

'Even if,' she whispered as his being engulfed hers and the thermonuclear reaction of matter and antimatter fusion sparked and began to eradicate them both, 'our puny existence, the conclusion of an agitated, conscious universe, is insignificant, dear love, I believe that mercy will go on. Kindness will go on.'

Let there be gentleness, she thought. Let there be equilibrium, if all there is and will be can survive in some form. Let there be grace and goodness and a hint of something to come, no matter how uncertain.

Let there be *possibility*, she thought, as they flickered and were immolated in some fool's idea of love.

For the 145 innocents of the 16/12 Peshawar terrorist attack and countless known and unknown before.

IN THE RUINS OF MOHENJO-DARO

Look for the ghost trees, memsaab, the college chowkidar had told Noor, grinning from ear to ear, and indeed the road to Mohenjo-Daro was lined with them. Rows of acacia, jand, and Indian lilac stood shrouded in clouds the colour of steel filigree. Noor pressed her nose to the window, watching the treetops blur and disappear in the half-breathing ether. The November dawn was clear, not a hint of fog, but the grey clouds stretched their amoebic limbs in either direction mile upon mile as if the Sind riverbank was haunted by a limitless phantom coiled around the foliage. When the school bus sped past one such tree, the wind rush pulsed the spectre until it filled with sunrise. Branches red-dark emerged in glistening veins.

Locust swarms, insect hordes, cotton candy – Noor's brain groped for an explanation. Sunlight twitched in one of the cocooned trees and the illusion of giant blood corpuscles recurred. Noor's vision misted; her temple sizzled. For a moment she feared the onset of a cluster headache. The last was two months ago right after she joined the cadet college. It had disabled her for two days. Now was not the time for another.

She stretched her neck from side to side, and flinched when Junaid touched her shoulder. The headache flared. Angry, she turned towards him. His starched white collar jutted into his neck. The striped red tie with the cadet college crest – crossed scimitars underlaid by pine boughs, surrounded by a half moon – looked uncomfortable, but he was beaming, brown eyes sharp and arrogant. He jabbed a stubby finger past her face.

'Spiders,' he said and widened his thin lips.

'Don't touch me again,' Noor said, voice cold as glass. When he continued to grin, she looked to the roadside. White crab spiders – hundreds of them dangling in the gossamer mass blooming from the trees. Gently they swayed in the wind, milky beads studding the latticework – which she now realized was webbing.

'Have you seen any flies or mosquitoes since you came, Miss Hamdani?' Junaid's hand rose crablike to sprawl on the headrest in front of her. 'The locals told me this happened after all that flooding last year. Thousands of spiders took refuge in the trees.'

From the corner of her eye she watched him finger a strip of leather peeling off the seat. His nails were perfectly manicured. He tore off the strip, drew it into his mouth, and spoke around it, 'Everyone was worried about malaria outbreaks. Guess the ghost trees took care of that,' and when Noor didn't respond, 'What? Don't tell me you're still angry.'

'I'm not,' she said sharply.

'Come now. It's Eid. Let's be festive and forgiving.' He was sitting next to her in a row three seats wide and his breath stirred the edge of her hijab. She edged closer to the window. He began to chew the leather strip. 'Kids are watching. Have to be model teachers now, don't we?'

Good point, asshole, she thought and closed her eyes. Not that she needed a reason to spurn his advances. This display of dickhood wasn't limited to him. Several of the faculty – all male except for a quiet burkah-clad part-time lecturer, who disappeared as soon as her classes were over, and Tabinda who now sat left of Junaid in the third seat – leered at her during morning assembly and talked down to her at lunch. Most were graduates of cadet colleges and had carried the attitude into their professional lives. That she taught English in an American accent hardened their condescension for some reason.

Her students didn't seem to care. They were clearly not used to female teachers, her hijab gained her some respect, something she'd seen frequently in this area. Part of the rural tradition, she supposed. She wondered how they would react if she whipped out Oxford jeans and white shirts, her preferred dress back in her high school days in New Hampshire, instead of the shalwar kameez and dopatta she wore now.

She glanced at the boys. They'd set out raucous and excited at predawn, but the motion of the bus had lulled them and they were dozing. Twelve teenage cadets, heads back, eyes closed, athletic arms crossed over their chests or dangling off the armrest. Dara, the tall, muscular kid with sharp green Pashtun eyes was awake, however, and staring at her. She nodded to him. He looked away.

There's another friend I made, Noor thought and covered her smile with a hand.

About half past ten they entered Dokri. Junaid pointed out Cadet College Larkana to the boys as they passed it: a pink structure flanked by red brick wings and triangular arches opening on to the first- and second-floor classrooms. A cast iron gate blocked the driveway leading up to the school building.

'This is *my* alma mater. Hundreds of acres. Large grounds, several football and hockey fields,' Junaid announced. 'We'll stop here on the way back if you like.'

They left the town with its streets bustling with cloth merchants, labourers and food vendors. Noor watched the last of the driver-hotels disappear in the distance and, as always when leaving a town, was filled with loneliness, an incomprehensible nostalgia she couldn't displace no matter how hard she tried.

The feeling lasted until they stopped 10 minutes later to fuel up at a small, peeling gas station, and the boys poured out to use the restroom and grab snacks from the mart. While Junaid and the bus driver chatted up the pump attendant, Noor slipped away. She stood behind a row of ghost cypresses and poplars along the riverbank and watched the smoke from her Marlboro Light spiral its way through the spider cocoon swaying above her. Dozens of insects hung dead or twitching in it. Hundreds of eyes glinted. If she reached out with her cigarette, could she set the whole thing ablaze?

'Quite a sight, isn't it,' said a familiar voice.

Noor snuffed out the Marlboro on the nearest tree bark before turning. Tabinda leaned against a poplar, gazing thoughtfully at the water shining through gaps in the verdure.

'Cigarette?' Noor said. She'd never seen the professor smoke.

Tabinda smiled. She was a plump woman in her sixties with a bovine face and horn-rimmed glasses. Her teeth were rotten but her smile reached her eyes. 'That shit you smoke? Nah.' She thrust a chubby hand at Noor as if offering to shake. 'Look at my hand. Near the wrist. See where the two tendons join? It used to be easier to find when I was thinner, but can you see the dip in the skin?'

Noor looked at the concavity at the base of the woman's thumb, where it met the wrist. The skin was tinged orange, and pale compared to the dark brown surrounding it.

'That's called the anatomical snuffbox.' Tabinda lowered her hand. 'I was addicted to homegrown tobacco in my younger days, see? Place a pinch there and snuff it right up. Quit about ten years ago when my doctor found a spot in my mouth. He took it out, biopsied it. Turned out it was pre-cancerous. And that was the end of that.' She nodded to herself and turned back to the river.

Noor watched the sun paint the woman's cheek golden. They'd talked a few times before. Shared a few details about families. Noor told her about her mother back in the U.S. and how long it had been since she had seen her. How difficult it was to live a transplanted life. Tabinda told her about her marriage to a wife beater in Lahore and how she escaped by divorcing and moving a thousand miles away to teach Pakistan Studies in Petaro. Commiserated about Noor's transfer from Karachi to this 'shit-hole town,' as she put it. Tabinda had a Punjabi accent and a nasal voice. Noor found it easy to like her; she was so jaded and sassy.

'Looking forward to exploring the ruins, Miss Hamdani?' said Tabinda.

'Noor, please.'

'Noor. Sorry. At my age it's difficult to shed old habits. I'm used to calling all these men by last name.'

'Creates that distance, doesn't it?'

'Yes. Distance can be quite useful in this place.'

'When did you start working here?'

'Oh, about 15 years ago.'

'The faculty didn't...make you feel unwelcome?'

'Of course they did. That's what men do. But I also try not to get in their way.'

The rebuke was subtle but unmistakable. Noor stared between the moss-covered trunks at the bus across the road. 'What they were doing – it was wrong.'

'Bloodshed and sacrifice is a way of life here. Has been for centuries.'

'They don't know any better,' Noor said. 'I can't stand the sight of blood, but that wasn't why I stepped in. Teach kids to enjoy violence and they'll carry that lesson to the grave.'

Tabinda laughed. The sound was deep-throated and made her jowls jiggle. 'Half these cadets may be dead before 30. In their hearts they know it and it frightens them. Fear is the twin of anger and a cousin to arrogance.' She turned and walked towards the bus. She was agile for her age. Her voice carried back: 'This has always been a land of heroes and monsters, Miss Hamdani. Here you pick your battles.'

A soft wind soughed through the spider cloud, making the dead shudder. Insect dust pattered down on Noor's shoulders. She brushed it away. You're wrong, she wanted to say. This is exactly how it begins. Hand them a weapon and tell them to man up and that's the way to the mother lode of horror.

But, of course, she said nothing.

She had come upon them by accident the day before during her morning walk. The boy's name was Abar and he was holding the trussed goat down with his knees dug into its well-fed side. Two other boys Noor didn't know appeared and squatted to hold the goat's legs firmly. The animal – a tall, beautiful Rajanpur breed with spotted ears and a milky body – bleated and thwacked its head on the summer grass under the Kikar acacia. The sight made Noor's blood pound and she found herself stomping toward the trio.

'Hey,' she called across the football field. 'What do you think you're doing?'

The newcomers flinched and looked up, as boys do on hearing a voice of authority. Abar just smiled and jerked the goat's head back by the ears.

'Sir Junaid's orders,' he shouted and positioned the slaughter knife across the animal's throat. The blade glinted silver. It threw a dancing shadow across the green and Noor's vision rippled. For a moment she didn't know where she was, and anger swept over her.

'Put that goddamn knife down. *Now*!' She was 10 feet away and her voice boomed in the narrow grove of trees dividing the football and hockey grounds. Dropping the goat's legs, the newcomers sprinted away, but Abar didn't move. He pressed the animal's head down, an ugly grimace of anger and effort on his face.

'What's the matter, Miss Hamdani?' Junaid had materialized from behind the grove of trees. In his hands he held half a dozen steel skewers, a chopping knife, and a cutting block. Without taking his eyes off Noor, he set these next to the acacia and mopped his brow dramatically. 'How can we help you on this fine Eid day?'

'Did you ask the boys to do this?'

'Do what?'

'Slaughter animals on their own?'

He lifted his eyebrows in mock surprise. 'Yes?'

'Where's the butcher?'

'Sick. Off duty. Does it matter? It's sunnah to slaughter your own animals, isn't it?' He grinned at her. He had what her dad used to call a copstash: a thick wad of mustache that bristled at either end. It made him look like an extra in a TV show.

'Tell me again what the Prophet said about teaching mercy.'

He pointed at the goat. 'That is mutton. You eat it every day—'

'I'm vegan!'

'—and today's Eid. Someone has to slaughter the animal to commemorate Ibraham's gratitude to God for sparing his son's life. It could've been Ismael under that knife. Then we'd all be in a boatload of trouble butchering our sons and all, wouldn't we? All I'm doing is teaching my cadets to do it themselves. Very important learning to steel your heart.'

She wanted to punch him. 'They're kids! They need to learn kindness before cruelty.'

His eyes were chips of hot mica. 'Certainly not in these times. This is not cruelty.' He placed the skewers crisscross on the wooden block. 'It's necessity.'

Helpless, Noor glanced at Abar. The boy was smiling, a cold sneer that was frighteningly familiar. The feeling of unreality, of red-hot memory, resurged. Noor turned and strode away, blinking away the warmth in her eyes. Behind her rose the chant 'In the name of God…' and the animal was screaming, a loud gargling sound. If she kept walking, Noor thought, she could outpace the sound. Walk away before steam rises from the animal's throat in the winter air, before the red curtain drops in front of her eyes and the strange, staring faces emerge – one of which will be Muneer's. Always his.

As Noor fled, the sound was cut off suddenly.

Then there was chopping.

Through a thicket of trees they trundled into the low-lying areas of Mohenjo-Daro. In the distance the Sind River curled a blue finger around the plateau. Tabinda pointed out dull squat structures that formed the mounds on the ruins' outskirts.

'Pariahs lived in some of these,' she said.

The museum at Mohenjo-Daro was a red brick building with life-sized bronze replicas flanking its entrance. Two hundred meters away in the desolate sprawl of the ruins the Buddhist stupa rose from the giant mound like a skin-coloured tumour. Junaid and Tabinda disembarked to set up a picnic lunch, leaving Noor and the cadets to hurry into the museum.

'Had you come in spring,' said the curator, 'it would've taken you eight hours to get here from the college. You chose wisely. But, still, *this* late?'

Noor fingered the seated Priest-King statuette the curator had been showing the class, a tiny resin replica with pressed lips, closed eyes and a gouged nose. A crack ran down its forehead to the left cheek. 'Why? What happens in spring?'

The curator glanced at the wall clock. It was quarter past eleven. He scratched the crab-shaped mole on his cheek. 'The Sarwar Fair. Hundreds of pilgrims from villages all over the Indus Valley converge on the saint's tomb in the Baluchistan hills. They travel by foot and donkey carts and often clog up the roads all the way from Dadu to Sukkar. The soil of Sind is filled with miracles and magic.' His voice was monotonal as if he were reciting from a textbook.

Noor placed the resin figure on the counter. 'What time does the museum close?'

The man sighed. He was short and swarthy, dressed in a checkered ajrak shirt, white shalwar and an embroidered Sindi cap. His nametag said *Farooq*. As he looked at the mass of teenage boys loitering about the lobby, distaste crept into his face. 'Now.'

'It's not even noon.'

'It's Eid. We're usually closed for the holidays. I made an exception for the cadet college because I was told we'd be done by 10.'

'Oh.' She didn't know what to say. They had been delayed at a military checkpoint in Dadu. Apparently a suicide blast had occurred at a small mosque on the outskirts of Khairpur, killing an elderly women and her two grandchildren. The area was flooded by police and army personnel. Checkpoints had been established at various junctures from Larkana to their college at Petaro. The military was worried about a follow-up attack.

'Sorry,' she said to Farooq who was fingering his mole, 'but we travelled a long way for this. Most cadets go home during holidays, but they' – she pointed at the boys peering at clay urns in glass cases – 'had no one to take them. Either their families are away or they have no families. So a few of us volunteered—'

'Yes, yes.' Farooq waved his hand. 'Spare me heartbreaking accounts of army orphans. I'll give you a quick tour. Is this your entire party? Where's Ms Tabinda? She's the one who called me.'

Noor glanced at the entrance. Junaid and Tabinda were setting up lunch. She felt guilty that she couldn't help with such chores; her inability to speak Sindi prevented communication with the bus driver whose Urdu was rudimentary. She wished the professor, at least, could take the tour. The Mohenjo-Daro trip was her idea.

'Seems like we're it.'

Farooq nodded glumly. 'This way then. We'll start with the Memories of the Ancients display.'

She nudged the cadets and they followed him up the northern corridor.

His voice echoed as they passed through an arched doorway into a long hall flanked by glass cabinets on either side. 'Egypt, Mesopotamia and Indus Valley are the three earliest civilizations of the Old World – China came later – and all, of course, developed along water bodies. We used to believe they evolved and thrived in isolation, but now we know that Indus Valley and Mesopotamia traded with each other for centuries.' He pointed left and right at carnelian necklaces, sculptures, gemstone beads, ivory combs and brass containers with traces of herbal collyrium.

Noor's belly cramped suddenly. Period pains? But she wasn't due for another week. It would explain the headache she had earlier that morning. Wincing, she rubbed her abdomen.

'Discovered in 1922 by an officer of the Archaeological Survey of India, Mohenjo-Daro is thought to have been the most important city of the Indus Valley Civilization. Spread out over 250 acres on a series of mounds, its heyday was from 2500 to 1900 BC. It was suddenly abandoned then. No one knows why.'

Noor glanced over her shoulder. The kids looked suicidally bored. They drifted behind her, eyes glazed. The Pashtun boy Dara had his nose pressed against a cabinet, palms splayed against the glass, but she thought his reflected green stare was fixed on her. His biceps bulged on either side of his head.

'Most of Mohenjo-Daro lies underground. A Buddhist monastery was discovered atop the city's main citadel. You can still see the stupa. We don't know why the builders decided to erect it there hundreds of years after the city was abandoned. The mounds grew organically over centuries as people built platforms and walls for their houses. The name Mohenjo-Daro means "Mounds of the Dead" in Sindi.'

Farooq waved at a ceiling-high stucco wall covered with black-and-white and sepia photographs. A flicker of interest went through the cadets. They crowded around aerial and ground views of the ruins.

Noor had seen these in slideshows Tabinda put on before the trip. She went to Dara who hadn't moved. He edged left to allow her to lean against the cabinet. This close, he was taller than her. He smelled of sweat and cologne.

'I'm sorry about the other day,' she said in a low voice. 'I didn't mean to barge in on you two like that.'

The tips of Dara's brown ears darkened. She could see the tension in his bunched neck and shoulder muscles.

'And here,' boomed the curator's voice, 'is the most famous statue of Mohenjo-Daro. You might have seen the Priest-King's picture in textbooks on the Indus Civilization. This is a detailed replica of the original at the National Museum in Karachi.'

'It's okay. Really,' Noor told Dara. The boy's fingers had closed over the edge of the cabinet. 'I won't tell anyone. Some of my friends back in the US were like you. One of them was bullied and struggled with depression for years.' Her gaze went to the cadets gathered around the pictures. What would they do if they found out about this kid or his friend currently away during winter break? She didn't want to imagine. Seized by instinct, she lifted the corner of her hijab and hissed at him, 'We all have secrets. *Look*.'

His eyes flicked in her direction. They widened when he saw her left shoulder.

'Some think the Priest-King is neither a king nor a man. Some believe this is in fact a woman of considerable importance to the people of Mohenjo-Daro. A high priestess, may be, or a eunuch who led their religious rituals.'

'We all have secrets,' Noor said again. Dara looked at her with wary eyes. He was a backbencher, rarely said a word. His grades were average. She used to wonder if he was slow. She dropped her hijab into place.

Dara rapped a knuckle against the glass. His eyes were green fires. 'You don't know anything,' he whispered fiercely, turned, and fled down the hall.

She watched him go, then went to join the cadets peering at something in a glass case. Farooq glanced up as she approached.

'So glad you could join us.' He adjusted the Sindi cap on his head. 'I was just telling this young man about seal 34. Dr Gregory Fossel of University of Pennsylvania believes it represents a sacrifice ritual. Care to listen in?'

She watched him unlock the case and withdraw two artifacts. In one hand he held a reproduction of the tan soapstone seal. The boys murmured and jostled to get closer. A tall angular deity with a horned headdress and bangles on both arms stood atop a fig tree. With a gleeful face it looked down on a kneeling worshipper.

Nearby was a small stool on which lay a human head.

'Seal 34 is taken as evidence by some that human sacrifice was practiced as a fertility rite in this region. Similar to offerings to the goddess Kali in certain parts of India.'

Noor looked at the seal. Below the kneeling worshipper were a giant ram and seven figures in procession. They wore single-plumed headdresses, bangles and long skirts. The brutal and sombre sight chilled her. Her belly cramped again.

'Dr Fossel, however, has argued that the presence of Pashupati's seal' – Farooq held up the stone in his other hand. It showed a naked figure with three grim faces and ram horns seated on a stool surrounded by deer, rhinoceros, and elephants – 'means that the people of Indus had the option to proffer animals as substitute for humans.'

'Pashupati?' Someone chortled. Noor glanced up. It was Abar, the boy who had slaughtered the goat on Junaid's orders. He had a malicious grin on his face. 'What kind of faggot name is that?' He elbowed a friend.

'One of Shiva's names.' The curator glared at him. 'His incarnation as the Lord of Beasts.'

Both boys burst out laughing. A few others smiled.

'That's enough,' Noor told the boys. Giggling, they strolled down the hall. 'Sorry about that,' she said to Farooq.

His face was pinched and red. 'Forget it. That's the sort of kids we're raising now. Anyway, it's closing time.' Muttering, he led them back to the lobby.

At the exit, Noor flashed a smile and said, 'Thank you for the tour. Very educational.'

He nodded and made to shut the door.

'Every place has its secret flavour,' Noor said. 'Here's a question I always ask curators and guides.' She touched his sleeve. 'Tell us one thing about the site you normally wouldn't tell visitors.'

He looked at her with a cocked eyebrow. 'Lady, you're not from around here, are you?'

'That obvious, huh?'

'A local wouldn't ask me that question.' His gaze went over her shoulder. Past the verdigris-laced statue of the Dancing Girl of Mohenjo-Daro in a field by the entrance on to the rocky slope and beyond it. He stared at the citadel mound visible from the museum steps. 'What does it matter? I'll tell you *two* things,' he said. 'First: on the Day of the Goat, no one from Larkana district will stay in the ruins past dusk. Not even the watchman.'

'The Day of the Goat?'

'Second—' His eyes gleamed in the doorway. 'Why don't you ask Ms Tabinda about devil glass? Ask her why she and her crew stopped the restoration dig here in 2001.'

'What?' Noor stared at him, but he was already stepping back in, slamming the door, slipping the bolts and she was left on the doorstep with her cadets milling noisily about her.

They dipped sheermal in chicken-and-lentil soup and chased it down with yogurt lassi. Junaid described the strategic importance of the site's location near a body of water, but no one was interested. The cadets wanted to explore. Noor's eyes were riveted on Tabinda who quietly munched a piece of bread, her gaze never far from the ruins.

A cold wind followed them up the dusty gravel path winding between the citadel mound and lower town. Two miles west of the citadel was lush farmland. Odd that no dots of people speckled the furrowed fields. They hadn't seen any ox carts, motorbikes, or bicycles on the road leading into the city either. Noor assumed the labourers and farmhands had taken the day off for Eid. Her belly had settled and she felt more cheerful.

The farmland was separated from the salty sediment of the ruins by a levee. Tabinda said this was reinforced every year to help control annual flooding.

'Not that it always works. Last year heavy floods topped the levees and brought the white crab spiders out.' She smiled. 'The locals fear those spider trees, let me tell you. They think them a terrible omen.'

'An omen of what?'

'There's a folk tale about demon cattle that feed on the leaves of such trees. Some time ago Karachi University published a survey showing that in certain years coinciding with old Sindi lunar calendars, sacrificial activity intensifies in this region.' Tabinda rubbed her knuckles. 'The fact that the floods nearly destroyed the site last year doesn't help ease their minds about evil forewarnings.'

She was correct about the damage. By now the city proper had closed around them like a bony fist and the alley they walked was flanked by crumbling buildings topped with mud slurry for preservation. Windows gaped in brick houses laid in a perfect grid. Some houses had exterior staircases leading to the second floor and the steps were chipped and eroded. The city's smell hit Noor – salinity and dust, floodwater and age – and for a moment she felt as if she were falling, collapsing inside a claustrophobic funnel down into nothing. The feeling passed, leaving her slightly breathless.

The cadets began to meander. A few headed to the alley leading up to the citadel mound. Noor left Junaid to his attempts to herd them and strode to catch up with the professor walking briskly as ever.

'You didn't tell me you used to be an archaeologist,' she said.

Tabinda frowned. She was holding a palm against her mouth, two fingers pinching her nostrils. The edges of her eyelids behind her spectacles were pink. 'I hate this weather. Winter brings out all my allergies.' She sneezed and rubbed her nose. 'I'm not an archaeologist. I assume Farooq told you something. The man couldn't keep his mouth shut if you sealed it with mortar.'

She went up a stone staircase and lowered herself on to a platform jutting from the roof. Noor sat down beside her.

'He said you were involved with a dig here.'

'Yes. As consultant anthropologist. Greg Fossel and I were working on restoring parts of the site's drainage system. You'd be surprised at how extensive it was. One wondered why they went to such lengths for a city this small.' She dangled her legs back and forth, her face thoughtful. 'Then again, most of it remains underground according to sonar sweeping.'

'Why'd you stop?'

Tabinda drummed the edge of the platform. 'Circumstances.'

They gazed at the ruins sprawled around them. In the lower part of the city between copses of trees and rocks was more evidence of water damage: caving walls, piles of broken masonry, battered facades. Here and there the rubble twinkled.

Noor said, 'What did Farooq mean about devil glass?'

The professor's black eyes were inward. 'Vitrified pottery, of course. Sediment and relics turned to ceramic glass by extreme temperatures.'

'I don't understand.'

Tabinda laughed. The sound echoed in the alleys, as if it came from within the ruins. 'Why would you want to? It's only of interest to old farts like me.' She rose and made her way to the staircase.

'Why did he call it devil glass?'

Tabinda stood at the top step, her silhouette dark and bloated against the sun. She seemed to be transfixed by the ruins again. Behind her the stupa and the citadel mound reared against a winter sky devoid of birds.

'When the site was first discovered,' she said in a flat voice, 'the excavators found piles of glass spherules and silica chunks like those found in Libya and the Sahara. In some places large craters were present. It was assumed that either meteor impact or plasma discharges from lightning had melted the minerals. Fused soil into glass. None of which, of course, explains the hundreds of human skeletons lying bleached in the streets and alleys on top of the glass heaps.'

'What?' Noor pushed herself up from the ledge. Two streets away a cadet was pissing in the shadow of an ancient wall, his shalwar pooled around his ankles. She wanted to yell at him, but the urge was gone as suddenly as it had come. 'God. What killed them?'

'Who knows?' Tabinda shrugged, but did something flicker in the dark of her eyes? 'Carbon dating puts it around the same time the site was abandoned. The city didn't recover from the catastrophe. Whoever killed those people killed the entire civilization.'

A gust of wind swept Noor's hijab back and she stepped away from the platform, chilled and uneasy. Tabinda's fists were clenched by her sides.

She said *whoever*, not *whatever*, Noor thought.

'Come on, what happened here in 2001? You obviously have bad memories.'

'We lost three men. Superstitious labourers. One went mad and flung himself from the top of the citadel, died on the rocks. He wasn't quite *there*, to begin with. Another disappeared. The third tried to kill Fossel and was shot to death by the site watchmen.' Tabinda shivered. 'It was a dark year. And I had such nightmares.'

She gave Noor a tired smile. For the first time Noor noticed a mild droop to the left of her face. An old stroke or nerve palsy? The crease of flesh between her nose and lips was flat.

'So I left. Returned to Petaro. Rejoined the cadet college. I haven't looked back since.' Tabinda pushed her spectacles up her nose, squinted, pointed with a pudgy finger into the distance. Waving his hands in the air, Junaid walked in their direction. His arms looked strange and loose from up here, kameez sleeves ballooning and fluttering like desert birds.

Noor hesitated, then said, 'He probably wants us to start gathering the boys. We should leave.' Her stomach and flanks tingled. An insistent pressure surged through her lower abdomen. Early, but this was it, no doubt about it now. And she didn't even have pads.

Together they descended the stairs into the lengthening shadows of the city. Noor glanced at her watch. It was three in the afternoon.

Junaid finally caught up with them, panting and shaky. 'Why didn't you answer your phone?' he demanded, glaring at Tabinda.

'My purse is in the bus,' she said. 'Something happen?'

'We were just about to call the boys,' Noor said.

He shook his head. 'No. I don't want to create a situation.'

'What?'

His face was pale. 'Colonel Mahmud just called me. There was a terrorist attack at Cadet College Larkana. At least 50 armed men stormed the premises.'

'In Dokri?' Noor's hand went to her mouth. 'But we were just there this morning. Oh my God. Are people hurt?'

'Ten dead, and they're holding the survivors hostage. Two military contingents just left for the town. But that's not the worst of it. Army's got word that an attack's been planned on Petaro as well. They're targeting cadet schools.' His manicured fingers rubbed his throat. 'Mahmud doesn't want us to return. He wants us to stay here tonight and go to the Army base in Sukkar when the roads are cleared. Likely tomorrow.'

'Sukkar?' Tabinda's voice was full of incredulity. 'That's a hundred and fifty kilometres away. How will we get past Dokri? The road to Sukkar goes *through* the city!'

'I know. Don't you think I know that?' His voice was getting louder and a pair of cadets turned their heads.

'Lashkir-e-Jhangvi?' Tabinda said softly.

'No. Pakistani Taliban.'

'How far to Sukkar if we go south first and take a detour?' Noor said.

'Four hours by bus.'

And how many on foot? She imagined trudging on the

cracked, unpaved road under a moonless sky as night fell and surrounded them on all sides. The thought was unpleasant and ridiculous and she pushed it away. They had a bus and a bus driver, and these were cadets, not kindergarten kids.

'Did you talk to the driver?' Tabinda said. 'What did he say?'

'He wants to leave. He knows the area well and says he could take back roads, but problem is the goddamn Taliban' – he spat in the dust – 'have spies everywhere. If we're on the road, they will know. Mahmud doesn't want us to leave Mohenjo-Daro. There is an airstrip five kilometres west of here. Worst case: if the hostage situation doesn't clear up, he can call for a chopper to airlift us out.'

Stuck in the ruins. Noor cast a glance at Tabinda. Her face was a mask.

'It's cold but there are blankets in the bus, and food, and I can get a fire going. We'll tell the boys it's an Eid bonfire. Dammit,' he said through gritted teeth. 'I want to be in Dokri with the Army. Larkana's *my* school!'

'Our first responsibility is to the students, don't you think?' Tabinda said. 'Besides, you wouldn't leave two women alone with a dozen kids in this place, would you?'

His fingers tugged at his mustache. The ends bristled. 'I guess not.'

'Good. We need to stay calm and think this through.'

'Don't tell me to be calm. I am calm.'

'Of course you are,' Tabinda enunciated each word and Noor looked at her again. The professor had steel in her eyes. Her lips twitched when she smiled at Junaid. 'Tell you what, see the citadel mound? It used to be a giant communal bath for the city. There's a grotto right below it. Good place for a fire pit. Why don't you get one going there? I have chickpeas and nuts. We can roast 'em and tell ghost stories and pretend we're on a camping trip.'

Junaid's eyes were riveted on Tabinda. The panic had left his face and the mean, arrogant look had returned. 'Don't you fucking patronize me, you hear?' He swivelled on his heel and stalked off towards the bus.

Tabinda watched him go then turned to Noor. Her cheeks were blanched, the facial droop more pronounced. 'This is bad.'

'Yes.'

'This is very bad,' Tabinda said, and licked her lips. 'We shouldn't be here after dusk.'

Again that feeling, that sensation of her mind separating from her body and eddying down a dusty funnel. Noor's head blazed, pain streaking through her like a dull saw. Dizzy and nauseated, she shot out a hand to clutch a nearby wall.

'...okay?' Tabinda was saying.

Noor leaned against the wall. 'I think so.'

'What happened?'

'I don't know.' She tried to control her breathing and it whistled down her throat. 'I get cluster headaches sometimes. May be it's my period triggering it.' She massaged her temples with both hands. Her right eye was beginning to water. 'What are we going to tell the kids?'

'We'll think of something. Let's go before they think the city swallowed us alive.'

They trekked between the city walls, corralling boys along the way, so many boys. Were there really only a dozen? Noor felt as if there were more – jumping, dashing, peering out from behind uneven walls, skidding through the dust. Other tourists? She hadn't seen any vehicles except for the site watchman's bike in the gravel lot. Certainly the two figures – so tall their heads brushed against the doorframe – who goggled at her from one of the houses then danced back into the gloom were not her boys.

She rubbed her eye and continued walking until they reached the bus. Junaid and the bus driver, Hamid, were talking. They fell silent when the cadets approached, but Noor didn't miss the uneasiness in the driver's face and the way he muttered when he thought no one was looking his way.

'Is Hamid from around here?' Noor asked Tabinda as the kids settled around the heap of firewood.

'The driver? Don't know. Why?'

'Just wondering. He didn't seem too keen on staying here tonight.'

'He can join the club,' Tabinda said. She was squatting next to the Pashtun boy, Dara, her back to the citadel's eastern wall. The structure towered above them, its shadow pawing the network of alleys that branched and twisted into the city's labyrinthine heart. They were shelling chickpeas and walnuts and tossing the husks into a metal bowl. Dara had wandered over after Noor and Tabinda cleared chips of masonry and rocks from the excavated grotto and volunteered to help. He kept his eyes away from Noor's, but she was glad to see him.

She looked across the plateau to the bus parked in the visitor lot and was startled at how dusk had whittled the day down to an unsettling purple. The shadows were long and jagged. She could hardly make out the driver carrying stacks of blankets from the bus. He and Junaid had roused the cadets into two scavenging teams and they had piled twigs with kindling on top. Noor doubted it would last more than a few hours, but it was better than nothing. Most boys had school cardigans on anyway and blankets would serve the rest. The remains of the picnic basket were spread out. Kinnows and apples. Peanuts, walnuts and chickpeas ready to be roasted. Really they were all set to face the cold night.

So why this uneasiness in her body? Her bones felt knobby and sharp against the stony ground.

Junaid knelt down by Tabinda. 'Is your phone working?' he said in a low voice.

'What do you mean?' she said.

'Is your damn phone *working*? I can't reach Mahmud.'

Tabinda flicked a peanut shell into the bowl and pulled her Nokia out. She peered at it, raised it high, and frowned. 'That's strange. I have no signal bars. '

'Me neither. I can't reach anyone.'

'Weather, you think?'

Junaid lifted a hand and scratched his cheek. 'It's not raining, and there's been no storm.'

Tabinda's eyes widened. 'No!'

Junaid nodded.

'What?' Noor said.

Junaid looked at Dara, who was quietly peeling nuts, and got up. Noor understood. Rubbing her hands together, she rose and followed him until they were a safe distance away.

'They blew up the signal towers,' Junaid said without preamble.

Noor stared at him. 'What?'

'Cellular base stations. The closest is in Dokri with a network of small booster towers along the way. I'll bet you anything most of them are gone. Which means the fighting is closer than I thought.' He sagged a little. 'We're stuck here unless they send an air carrier. Or we can drive back.'

'You're saying we should?'

'No. We don't know what's going on out there. At the moment this place is safer.'

Noor opened her mouth, closed it. Her gaze went to the vast, empty buildings towering above her. It was dark now, the sun just a blood smear on the horizon, and the houses of Mohenjo-Daro pressed together. Broken platforms poked and plunged; holes gaped in the walls. Above, an icteric moon sat distorted by a low cloudbank, its light not a promise, but the barest hint of a possibility.

'We've got to tell the kids now,' she said.

'Yes.'

Noor shifted her weight. The icy evening wind cut through her shawl and she shivered. Her abdomen tensed. She hadn't begun bleeding yet, but she would soon.

'Let's get it over with,' she said.

They returned to the bonfire. The cadets gathered around and listened to Junaid. Their faces showed shock and delight at this new development. Spend the night in the ruins! Eagerly they asked how long the trouble would last.

'We don't know yet.' Junaid shook his head. 'We'll just have to be patient.'

They left the boys chattering and went to the bus where Hamid the bus driver was talking with the site watchman, a bald, paunchy man with a pockmarked face. The watchman swept a hand toward the mounds and it triggered another round of debate between the two.

'What's going on?' Noor said.

Hamid lifted his head. He was tall and very gangly, features filed by several summers spent in this unforgiving land. He wore a khaddar chador around his shoulders in the fashion of northern Pashtuns. He stared at Noor through narrowed, kohl-lined eyes, then turned to Junaid and spoke rapidly in Sindi.

'What's he saying?'

Junaid pressed his hands together. Slowly he began to crack his knuckles. 'He says the watchman wants us to leave. Hamid's leaving, too, and won't be back for three days.'

The museum curator was right. The locals didn't linger here on…what had Farooq said? The Day of the Goat. Noor looked at Tabinda who was studying the darkening sky.

'Why?'

'They don't like this place at night.'

The watchman muttered something and even in the moonlight Noor saw colour drain from the bus driver's face. He whispered to Junaid who retorted angrily. Two cadets who'd followed them giggled.

'Chario Hamid. Geedi Hamid,' they cried.

Noor knew 'geedi'. They were calling him a coward. Hamid yelled at them and they laughed and skipped away. Noor didn't like the sound of that laughter; it had a tinge of hysteria about it. Hamid and the watchman stood together, their faces stubborn and scared.

'Mu'al' raat jo sujjhi pawanda,' said the watchman, and Hamid flinched.

'Will you please tell me what they're saying?' Noor hissed at Junaid.

'Rubbish.' He looked at the top right corner of his cellphone's screen and grimaced. 'The dead swell here tonight,' he muttered. 'What fucking nonsense.'

The cold was making Noor's skin tingle. She glanced at Tabinda, who was looking away at the silent and antediluvian ruins. Hamid said something and Junaid snapped at him. The driver threw up his hands. The watchman closed his fist then flung his fingers out at Junaid, a gesture that needed no translation: *Go to hell.*

The watchman turned and disappeared behind the mounds.

Hamid glared at the three of them. Spitting in Sindi, he climbed on to the bus, turned the key and began revving the accelerator.

'Is he leaving?' Noor said, alarmed.

Junaid looked furious and helpless. 'Yes. If we don't go now, he'll leave without us. We've got to gather everyone.'

The fire was guttering when they reached the cadets. Wood crackled. The shadow thrown by the flames turned the boys' faces sly when Junaid announced they were leaving.

'We can't go yet,' said a freckled rat-faced boy named Tabrez, whom Noor recognized as part of Abar's posse. 'We need to wait.'

'What do you mean?' Junaid said sharply. 'Wait for whom?'

The boy popped a handful of roasted chickpeas into his mouth. Crunched them. 'They said they'd read about a secret room in the ruins. Went treasure hunting, Abar and Raheem.' Seeing Junaid's aghast expression, he smiled sweetly and added: 'Don't worry. They have torches and shovels.'

A mile from the city in a narrow ditch between two rocks Noor undid the nala string, lowered her shalwar, and squatted. She put a hand between her legs, brought it out and stared at the viscous stain glisten in the flashlight's glow.

Blood.

The smell was stronger than usual. Fishy. Perhaps it was the air down here. She wiped her hand on the rock, leaving a print with beetles squirming in the digits, and waited for the flow to abate. She finished up with paper napkins and water from a bottle then rose and, one finger scratching beneath her hijab, she stood watching the dot of fire amidst the mounds.

She had shown Dara her scars, the raw pink-white ridges coiling serpentine around her collarbone and shoulder, and was filled with amazement at her daring. She'd never shown them to anyone, not even cheery, gentle Mark with whom she spent a night in Hanover before she left for Pakistan. Her lawyer had appealed for repatriation and to everyone's surprise – most of all, her own – succeeded. She supposed it made sense. She'd never been charged and couldn't be deemed guilty just by association. It was a frightening time, though, the last of her teenage years.

Mark. God, she hadn't thought about him in a decade, although in the beginning he was all Noor could think about. They had met at rehab soon after they released her. She was required to attend weekly sessions while arrangements were made. Mark was bipolar. Noor was benighted – terrified of what her past and future might bring. They had made love in darkness, his lips pressed to her neck, the comforting smell of his hair and body and his seed caustic to her senses; and if he noticed the roughness of her flesh or was dismayed by how she sobbed afterward, clutched her clothes, and fled – well, he didn't exactly call to ask about it.

The night wind gusted. Noor patted her hijab, tucked her kameez into place, and walked back to rejoin the group huddled by the fire.

Bent on one knee, Junaid held a lighter in one hand and a newspaper roll in the other. He clicked the wheel and a flame sprouted between his fingers. He touched it to the paper roll. A red-hot tongue of fire whooshed to life and began to devour the paper.

'Did you find them?' Noor said.

He shook his head. 'It's a big place. They could be hiding anywhere. Although, when I do' – he gritted his teeth, thrust the burning roll into the dwindling flames and stirred the cinders with a twig – 'I'll beat them to a pulp, I swear.'

They had reached a compromise with Hamid: he would leave the bus behind and hitch a ride with the watchman to Baner, the nearest town. There, he'd try to contact and update Colonel Mahmud on their situation as well as find out details of the confrontation between the military and the militants.

'I really wish you would all come with me,' he told Junaid in Sindi before hopping on the bike, but that was impossible. Abar and Raheem were still missing.

'Sir Junaid,' a cadet said. 'May we have some more sheermal? We're hungry.'

'In a bit,' he said, then whispered to Tabinda, 'How much food is left?'

'Another meal. May be two if we're stingy. We didn't prepare for this.' She raised her palms to the fire, then shouted, 'Who wants to tell ghost stories?'

'Me,' called someone. 'What a mummy-daddy,' said another.

Gathered around the flames, ignoring the thrumming black, cold licking their flesh, they told stories. Tall tales that became stranger and stranger:

A silent ugly schoolboy bullied by his classmates is wrestled and stripped and thrown to the ground. He turns into a horned beetle, burrows into the earth. Returns night after night as a monstrous insect with a boy's face, peering into his tormentors' windows, tapping and chirping, until they go mad from lack of sleep.

A man on a lonely mountain road comes upon a goat, decides to steal it and carry it home – only to find the animal growing heavy on his back, its limbs elongating, cleft hooves dropping until they drag on the ground. The thief throws the animal off and flees, and monstrous laughter chases him all the way home.

The soot-covered raven man flitting from tree to tree in a Hindu cremation ground.

The pregnant woman in the bushes with snake tresses and backward feet.

A knot of wood exploded in the fire and an ember landed between Noor's legs, startling her. She toed it out with her sneaker, shook the stiffness from her back. She opened her mouth to ask if anyone wanted another blanket. 'I know a good one,' she said instead, and blinked with surprise.

They turned, fire-lit faces pale and sombre. Eyes rheumy from smoke and ash stared at her.

'My mother was a teacher at a Jewish centre in America,' she said. 'She told me the Yom Kippur story of the Sent Goat. It scared me witless as a child. Have you heard it?'

They shook their head.

'In the old days the Israelites performed a rite called the *se'ir mishtale'ach* on the Day of Atonement. Two goats were selected in a ceremony. Healthy, unblemished specimens. Lots were drawn over them: on one was written "Lord", on the other "Azazel". The goat whose lot drew "Lord" was slaughtered immediately as atonement for the nation's crimes that year. The other…' She looked around the campfire, at their reddened, glassy eyes and quivering mouths. 'Anyone know what *Azazel* means?'

'Yes,' Tabinda murmured. She was sitting next to Noor, her hands knotted together in her lap. 'A demon of the wilderness.'

'That's correct.' Noor nodded. 'The second goat was sent into the desert, supposedly laden with the sins of Israel, to Azazel the wild demon, the pagan god waiting to devour it. Azazel also translates as "the goat that departs". The word *scapegoat* in English comes from this ritual. The animal sacrifice and exile were symbolic of what might happen to an unrepentant tribesman. This was how they made themselves feel better.' She smiled bitterly. 'Sound familiar?'

The cadets' faces were masks dappled orange and black. They watched Noor with unflinching eyes. The freckled boy, Tabrez, leaned and whispered in his neighbour's ear, and they both giggled.

'That's a horrible story,' Junaid said. His teeth gleamed in the firelight like a serrated blade. 'I didn't know you were so twisted, Miss Hamdani.'

He wet his lips and grinned. His hand moved slowly to his lap. Was he turned on? She felt frigid and tired, and grateful when Dara got up and brought more tinder.

Tabrez whined and Tabinda handed out four foil-wrapped packets of sheermal. They disappeared quickly. Someone wondered why Abar and Raheem weren't back; perhaps a small group could go look for them in the ruins. Tabinda said 'No!' so forcefully it startled them into silence.

Junaid stared at her and said he was sure they'd be back when they got hungry.

The fire whooshed and retreated from the night and Junaid and Dara piled on more wood. A couple of cadets laid out their blankets near the fire. Before they could settle in, from beyond the looming citadel came scraping sounds.

Pebbles rolled.

Someone was walking the dark near the Buddhist stupa.

They glanced up. Just a black sky crinkled with a faint yellow moon.

In the distance a door swung open on screeching hinges. A shout and a crash.

'Abar,' yelled Junaid, springing to his feet. 'Is that you?'

A cadet screamed and shrank back from a night-thickened alley 20 feet away, where a tall figure jutted its face. It spasmed briefly, rotating its arms above its head – glass bangles glinted – and vanished. Pounding of boots on stony ground. In the ruins someone laughed, the shrill and birdlike sound overlaying the running footsteps until both faded. Junaid shouted the boys' names again and plunged into the dark beyond the fire, the halo from his flashlight jittering up and down the streets.

A sound came from beside Noor. She turned. Tabinda's face was doughy, a faint twitch at the left corner of her lips. Her forehead glistened with moisture. Her hand was at her throat, massaging it.

She's sweating, Noor thought. In this cold.

An unfamiliar dry smell flooded her nose, triggering memories that disappeared before she could seize them, leaving her breathless and frightened. A sudden raging headache made her eyes tear. Tabinda whispered – so softly Noor doubted anyone else heard. The words made the hair on the back of her neck stand. She would remember them later, like a dream song or a grief prayer running over and over in her head, as the derelict city rustled and the river-stink of fish and reeds and dead gelatinous creatures crept into her nostrils.

'He opens his mouth so,' said Tabinda. 'The Terrible Emperor of the Night.'

The cadets held hands, bleary eyes peering in every direction, finding ancient houses entombed in night; narrow alleys mazing in black – empty of life, yet something stirred. Somewhere in the ruins Junaid stumbled, crashed, and cursed, before falling silent.

'What's happening, Miss?' cried one of the boys.

'To the bus,' Noor hissed. 'Now.'

They gaped at her before turning. Falling over each other, they covered the distance to the bus in seconds, piled in, burrowed into their seats. Once Tabinda was on board, Noor slammed the lock home. They stared at the distant mounds gleaming in the moonlight like tombstones.

'What was that?' said a cadet in a hitching voice.

'Someone turn on the light,' said another.

'No!'

'Abar and Raheem,' Noor said. 'Lost and calling for help.'

'Are you fucking kidding me?' Tabrez said incredulously. 'That was laughter.'

'Watch your language.'

'Did you not hear it?' He leaned his forehead against the window and gazed at the bonfire wavering by the citadel. 'That didn't even sound human.'

'I shouldn't have returned. I thought, I thought… I was *wrong*,' Tabinda cried. She had sagged into a back seat. Her hands, like small animals, were hiding beneath her thighs.

Noor swallowed. Her lips were parched.

'An animal. A jackal perhaps,' she said.

Tabrez said. 'Who was that man in the alley?'

The Terrible Emperor of the Night, Noor thought. She didn't have the energy to grope her way to Tabinda, ask her what she meant. The woman had sunk into her seat, head lolling on her breasts like a rotten fruit.

Noor took stock of the water bottles under the bench behind the driver's seat. Two twenty-four packs. She removed one, drank from it, passed it around. Someone made a choking sound then fell silent. Noor raised a fist and knuckled her throbbing temple.

Tabrez rapped at the window with his knuckles. Someone told him to shut the fuck up. He gave them the finger before resuming: Tap tap!

They waited for Junaid. Their breath misted the windshield glass and white sheathed it until their reflection disappeared.

Tap tap. Tap tap tap.

Sheermal was handed around again. Noor declined the bread. An odd lethargy had settled on her. The kids chewed, filling the bus with sounds of gnashing teeth and crumpling aluminum. Noor's neck ached as if steel rivets were being driven into it. The pain exhausted her. Her eyelids drooped.

Noor fell into sleep.

She was a teenager. Dressed in a black shirt, blue jeans and leather boots, she stood in the middle of Mohenjo-Daro with a bomb vest strapped under her clothes. Her hair whiplashed in the hot desert breeze. Her gaze was fixed on the citadel – now shaped like Port Authority Bus Terminal in New York, stripes of neon blue and red racing around its sides. Noor's finger caressed the trigger poking her flat stomach.

A finger prodded her in the back. Muneer. He was young and sallow, exactly like she remembered him. Eyes large and white from thyroid proptosis.

'For Dad,' he said, voice guttural, toad-like. He pointed a long fingernail at hundreds of skeletal men, women and children twitching their way through sun-baked alleys. They wore business suits, sweatshirts, dresses and tourist caps. Suitcases and backpacks dangled from bones picked clean by time. They converged at the terminal like pilgrims at the Kaaba, pawing at the steel armature, phalanges digging into bricks, clenched fists thudding on glass.

'For their sins. Go, little sister, go.' Muneer's bulging eyes made him look shocked and insane. 'Soon I will join you.'

He shoved her forward. Noor staggered and began to walk. The spectres of the city pounded on the terminal's walls, the half-flesh of their faces ruined, washed by electric colours blazing from the building's facade. Noor's vest was rough and heavy and it was difficult to breathe. Summer heat wringed sweat from her pores. Her finger itched.

I can't, she whispered. I don't want to.

But no one was listening, especially not God. Faith yanked her forward and Noor went on a loyal trot, getting closer to point zero. The crowd jittered to the tune of death. An infant drooped from his mother's shoulder and pulled her straggly hair; and in a minute there would be blood, there would be devastation.

Noor turned and bolted. The ground shifted beneath her. Muneer's face was everywhere. 'No, you bitch, come back. Geedi, geedi. *Coward!*' he screamed. The world was white noise and it hurt her head. She ran and ran. She would hide somewhere; if she could just reach safety, everything would be all right. No pain, no suffering, no dying, no shame, no guilt. Noor sprinted and the dead sprinted behind her, hundreds of taluses, tarsals and metatarsals rattling on the ground.

'Pashupati is dead, you miserable slut,' her brother sang. 'Now nothing will do but baby blood.'

Noor woke, shivering, to a freezing dark. The bus was quiet, the seats empty. Did Junaid return and take the kids elsewhere? Why wouldn't he wake her? Empty bottles, crumpled foil and sheermal crumbs littered the floor. Pulling her shawl tight around herself, Noor struggled upright. The windows were blinded with white. For a moment she thought they were covered with snow, like her bedroom window back in Hanover used to be after a winter storm. Dad would clear it, his gloved hands patting the frost off.

But Dad was gone. *Extraordinary rendition*, her lawyer called it.

A closer look revealed the white as fog. Thick smoky layers pressed against the glass, consuming the bus. Sometime during the night it had crept in from the river. She glanced at her watch. It was just past midnight.

She wanted to turn the headlights on but was afraid of what she might see. The dream hadn't left her yet. At least her headache was gone. She made her way to the exit and peered out: white upon pristine white. Wasn't white the sum of all colours? Was it Goethe who said colour itself was a degree of darkness? She couldn't see three feet away. There was a metallic tang in her mouth as if she could taste the vapour.

'Junaid,' she yelled. Instantly the fog devoured the cry. 'Abar. Tabinda. Anyone.'

No answer. Just a susurration of dust and weeds in the wind. No night birds sang, no insects chirped. She was blind and alone. Terror came then on dark wings, whelming her heart. She shoved it away, though her stomach and bladder quivered. How could she not have heard them leave?

She clicked an overhead light on. The glow spread like a thin puddle. Her brown eyes were wide and crimson-webbed in the rearview mirror. Her hijab had fallen off and lay draped over her shoulder. Noor fixed it with trembling fingers.

May be she should drive away. Leave them all here. The thought was so powerful she actually took a couple steps toward the driver's seat before stopping. There was no key in the ignition. Junaid had it, of course. Movement in the periphery of her vision made her turn.

The bus door had slid open. Tabinda stood in the doorway, a rotund silhouette with streams of fog snaking between her ankles. 'I came back for you,' she said.

Noor wanted to weep for joy. She ran and flung herself at the older woman. Tabinda's arms tightened around her. 'Sorry. The kids were cold and you were sleeping.'

'Where are they now?'

'In a warm place.'

Noor squeezed her once more and stepped back. 'Let's go. Have you seen Junaid?'

Tabinda shook her head. 'No.' Her face was half-paralysed now. The corner of her mouth sagged. Her left eye was half-lidded.

'Are you all right?'

Tabinda massaged her cheek. 'I had a stroke some years back. This happens once in a great while.'

'Were you here in the ruins when you had the stroke?' Noor said. The question came to her familiarly, as if she'd asked this before in a dream.

Tabinda's lips had cracked from cold. They bled a little when she tried to smile.

'How did you know?' She held the door open. 'Should we get going?'

They strode through air dense as a blizzard. Noor couldn't understand how Tabinda kept her bearings. Shadows heaved and parted before them. They stepped on twigs, nettles, sharp rocks. The fog sucked its breath in, exhaled and rushed past. When the texture of the ground changed, Noor knew they were on the city streets. Broken masonry crunched underfoot. Stones, brick shards, gum wrappers, a worker's implement. At least that's what she thought it was. Long and pale, it gleamed in the moonlight. Before Noor could bend to examine it, her companion took her hand and pulled her. 'This way.'

Tabinda scythed the haze with an outstretched arm. They approached a towering structure. The Buddhist stupa. Noor put her hand out and scraped a fingernail across the wall. How cold and brooding and alien it felt with misty vapours clinging to it. She remembered her dream – shiny white phalanges groping the building – and her stomach turned. She pinched her shalwar and rubbed the brick dust off.

'I liked your little history lesson,' Tabinda said. 'But it has more meaning than the Israelites gave it.'

'What?'

'It describes existence accurately. The two goats are

life and death, equally horrendous conditions. Gods are vindictive, after all. Would you like to hear another story? It's from the Mahabharata.'

Noor hesitated, then said, 'Sure.'

'In the beginning were three cities that orbited the earth. They were not happy places.'

In the distance vibration rose, faint as insect static. Noor cocked her head. It was coming from beyond the citadel deep in the night.

'What's that?'

'The cities fought each other with iron thunderbolts smelted in a hundred thousand suns. Until one invented a unique weapon.'

Tabinda stopped. Before them was a twisted iron door flanked by massive brick colonnades. Rust blanketed it from top to bottom, except for the emblem of the Dancing Girl, hand on her hip, stamped in the middle. Parts of the figure were eroded by age, but even through the fog the dancer's eyes, open and swollen with madness, were visible. A brass padlock dangled from a moon-shaped hasp. The door was ajar.

'The weapon was wielded with the force of the universe behind it and it annihilated the rival cities. The cost of preparing it was grave, though. The inhabitants of the triumphant city had to use the blood of entire nations on Earth.'

Tabinda pushed the door and it screeched inward, trailing the vapour pall draped over it. She stepped back, letting Noor peer in. 'After you.'

Inside was blackness thick as blood. The noise in the sky was louder now. *Whack whack whack!* It sounded like a piece of meat stuck in the blades of an electric fan.

'What *is* that?' Noor said uneasily.

The professor stood enshrouded in white, her uneven face glassy and still as a pool. 'It's the Army chopper come looking for us,' she said. 'Don't worry. They can't land in this fog.'

Noor tried to back out, but Tabinda was quick. A two-handed fist slammed Noor's shoulder blade. Agony shot through her spine, buckling her, sending her flying through the doorway. Blackness rushed at her. She flailed her arms, trying to grab a handhold but tripped and smashed headlong into something solid. The world exploded into fractals: gray and black and grainy. A buzzing in her ears, something circling her brain, enfolding it like a reptile's maw – and Noor disintegrated.

Someone scraped up her pieces and put her together. She was slithering down steps as cold and unforgiving as faith's hold. Liquid heat simmered in her eyes. Her knees bumped and banged. One shoe jammed in a crack at the edge of the staircase; someone yanked her foot out and continued dragging her.

She was placed on a hard surface. Mist and incense

smoke roiled in a vortex around her. Her eyes watered from the fumes. Through the haze she glimpsed figures revolving slowly. Half a dozen, may be more. They drummed long spear-like objects on their sneakers and boots.

Noor licked her lips. Her tongue was a festering ulcer, her head a beehive of bewilderment. Pain squeezed her shoulders when she raised her head. She moaned. She was lying on her stomach on a narrow ledge inside the citadel, a long rectangular room with a brick ledge running from end to end three feet above the dry communal pool. The great bathhouse. It took her a minute to realize that her wrists were throbbing. They were bound with rope. So were her ankles.

'For a long time I wondered why the inhabitants of Mohenjo-Daro were so particular about the drainage system,' said Tabinda. She was standing in the middle of the pool before a brick-lined circular opening about six feet wide. Mist wreathed the hole and Noor couldn't see inside it. Tabinda wore a fan-shaped metal headdress with its edges dipped to create circular indentations at both ends. Flames flickered in small clay lamps placed inside these hollows. Her face was red with heat and perspiration, the half-paralysis so bad it seemed she was scalded on one side.

'Every house had its own drain connected to a network of brick channels in the streets. The channels ran clever courses, ending here in the bathhouse. I couldn't understand why they'd want to dump sewage here. It didn't make sense.'

Tabinda was surrounded by a procession of seven figures:

cadets wearing bangles on their arms and circling diyas in the dense air. Smoke plumed in rapid spirals, thickening their features, sending sooty entrails across faces shining like glass. Tabrez and Raheem were among them. Tabrez's freckles glistened.

'It wasn't until Fossel and I unearthed the network of brick-lined conduits below the citadel that we understood the purpose of this extensive system.'

The seven boys began gyrating their way to the far end of the pool. Their eyes were glassy. Lamps flared and guttered in their hands. They disappeared in the murk. Noor's heart beat so fast she could feel her limbs jerk with every pulsation. Terror had driven the pain away.

'Even today the Indus script remains indecipherable to others, but Fossel said he had translated it. The meanings of the symbols came to him in a dream, he said.' A grotesque half-smile cracked the right side of her face. 'Inscriptions he found on seals described the inhabitants' belief in a supreme father. They called this deity the Terrible Emperor of the Night. Said that he ruled the meat-city in the sky with a lightning arm and a thunder fist, and that he had a hungry mouth on earth. Ancients in other cultures knew of this mouth. In their poems they called it the *os dhwosos*.'

She was mad. The woman was mad. Noor's blood was ice in her vessels. She strained at the ropes binding her, but it was futile. She arched her back and looked at her captors. Abar had materialized beside the professor. In his hand was a long piece of black glass the size of a child's femur – similar, Noor realized, to what she had glimpsed in the street. Devil glass. Abar's blank gaze was riveted on her. He ran a finger across the jagged edge of the weapon and it came away black with blood. Abar wiped it off on his school sweater. There was no cut.

'This wasn't a bathhouse, you see. This was an ablution pool,' Tabinda said gently, 'filled with the city's libation.'

It took Noor a moment to understand what that meant. When she did, her flesh went cold.

'Once a year the omphalos would tauten and the door to His house swing open. At some point, during years of drought and starvation perhaps, the people of the city turned to their children. Usually the oldest offspring lain and done by the blood gutters. It wasn't until enemy races conquered Mohenjo-Daro that the practice finally came to an end,' Tabinda said. 'The following year, however, in one night the entire city was destroyed along with its new rulers.'

The cadets reappeared, dragging a sizable bundle across the dry pool. It left a glistening black trail. A hand dropped from the bundle. Noor began to tremble, her breath hitching.

The fingertips were white, the nails perfectly manicured.

'How could've we known, you know, when we began the dig?' said Tabinda. Behind her Abar stood passing the glass knife from one hand to the other. It glimmered. 'I wanted to flee when the dreams started, but Fossel wouldn't hear of it. He wanted to study the darkness, as he put it. The tablets and seals indicated the secret room was real. And he said he would find it.'

They placed the bundle before the brick-lined drain. Tabinda stooped, rummaged and heaved out a lolling object. The oil lamp nearest her winked out. The bundle twitched and began to move. Noor gasped. Tabinda arched her neck to look at the sky. The incense smoke swirled a wreath around her head.

'After the labourers died, though, after the attempt on his life, Fossel was rattled to his core. He flew out the very next day. I left quickly myself. Spent years convincing myself it was a bout of madness. PTSD or some shit like that, but the nightmares just wouldn't stop. Every night the same voices, the same faces. This fucking room with its heaps of glass. Then I read about exposure therapy. Flood yourself with what you fear most. Sounds like a good idea, I thought. Return to the city on the anniversary of the day the horror began. Pop in, pop out, be done, never go back.'

Noor's bladder let go and wetness spread from her thighs to her navel. The cadets had begun to chant. The voices loud and synergistic in the murk rose higher and higher. 'Our blood Yours, our meat Yours. On this day gladly we give You our sins…'

Tabinda uttered a sudden sob. Her eyes were craters filled with fear and exhilaration. Abar stepped forward. 'Don't cry, slut. Don't you dare,' he said in a guttural voice that wasn't his. 'For this part, we steel our heart.' He handed her the knife. It nicked the hollow below her thumb and a drop of blood appeared. Tabinda held the glass knife high like a hammer. Her shoulders were quivering. The knife blade lashed out. A gurgling sound, and the bundle was thrashing. The perfect fingernails drummed. Tabinda's hand sawed back and forth and dark liquid gushed into the hole.

'He whose house is aboil. Adar Anshar. The Croucher in the Mounds. The Terrible Emperor of the Night.'

Noor was mute with fear. This wasn't happening. This couldn't be happening. She was at the college in Petaro, there had been an accident, and she was in a coma. She was still in the Burn Centre at New York Presbyterian after the blast. Her shoulder burns had become infected and she was delirious, watching her wounds glisten blue-green.

The cadets crooned and, throwing away the glass spears, gathered around her. Between them they hauled her to the edge of the hole, her bare feet chafing on the brick. Tabinda leaned back and wiped her forehead. In the lamp flame the liquid pouring down the hole was ochre. Tabinda murmured. Abar grabbed Noor's head and yanked it back. Fiery bits of glass impaled on metal skewers were jabbed into her nostrils. She struggled but it was futile. The smoke singed her sinuses, parched her tongue, flayed her throat. She gasped for water. A metal chalice was thrust into her hand and she drank eagerly, a grainy hot liquid that could have been molten glass or blood swirled with sand.

In this new state, this moiled clenching, Noor floated. Up she went, twisted into a spiral beguiling as the lines on a newborn's palm.

Below her were barren lands stripped by heat, their dwellers evolved into the formless. Towering mammoth structures squelched in magma. Half-buried in this boiling ground were giant hunchbacks whose humps formed the city's mounds. When they stirred, brackish fluid gushed through ciliated maps wavering from their flesh. The maps beat with an unnatural rhythm. Drawn from the hunchbacks' vasculature, they pumped pyroclastic liquid through the land's anatomy. A veined umbilical cord surged from the city centre, rising higher and higher, trembling through its singed sky, until it traversed it. The cord shot outward, connecting this world with a blue-green one.

My blood is Yours. My skin is Yours.

Noor splayed her hooves against the throbbing meat tunnel of this omphalos and crawled up-down inside it like a spider. She had three faces, equipoisal vision and a swollen belly. Her brother Muneer hung impaled on a giant claw on the opposite wall. His tongue was rotten, he was covered with sores. As she watched with a dozen eyes, he swelled suddenly and exploded.

Noor cried out. Her many limbs retracted, and she was falling, tumbling, plummeting, until she landed on a hard surface, shattering her extraneous appendages. A dense liquid clogged her airways. She couldn't breathe. She gasped and kicked and someone slapped her back, grabbed her hair and pulled her up.

Noor sat before the now-bubbling aperture, drenched in hot blood. Clots were already beginning to form in her hair. The citadel was dark except for the intermittent flare of oil lamps. The mist was thicker, the whirling of the procession speedier. She couldn't make out who they were, how many they were. She couldn't see Tabinda anywhere. The locus of the dance had shifted away from her to the other end of the pool.

Noor's hands and feet were still tied. Sobbing, she slid backward on her buttocks, turned, and began wriggling to the ledge like a worm. Faces glistening with blood protruded from the mist and disappeared. Hundreds of eyes blinked and died.

Someone touched her foot. Noor screamed. Images of that monstrous city swirled in her brain and her eyes bulged until a red curtain slipped over her vision – just like in the early days after Muneer's death. The smell of him, cooked from the blast, on her skin. The sharp iron of his blood. The taste of her own misery and terror as she stood shrieking in the summer wind, watching the red-and-white rain that was once her brother – they would come to her for months after she left the hospital.

Muneer died alone on that terrible day. She— She ran to a cop. Fled her murderous sibling and kept fleeing. But everywhere she had looked, since, was a skein of red death coiled like a mushroom cloud: in sultry evenings and in shadowy mornings, until she could hardly leave the house.

Her removal to Pakistan had been a relief.

The Pashtun boy Dara loomed above her. His face was covered with gashes and he had blood around his mouth. He put a finger to his lips – *sshh!* – and began to hack at the rope around her ankles with a glass knife.

The air thrummed. Voltaic ideograms crackled in the mist. A blue-black diagonal shimmered 20 feet away. A door set low and very wide. The oil lamps were clustered around it, flickering like fireflies.

Dara's hands dripped with sweat. A final swipe, and her feet were free. She couldn't believe it: she could move her legs. Sobbing with relief, she scrabbled on the ground until she was on her knees. Her period was starting again, a heavy flow, but she hardly noticed. It pooled around her feet and snaked toward the libation hole.

'Goat,' Dara said, his eyes dead and crimson. 'Depart, goat. Leave before He arrives.'

The knife moved to her wrists. Dara slashed at the rope until it gave. Noor tottered to a stand. The room tilted and her vision turned briefly foggy. A loud noise, like a door bursting open in the wind, came from behind her. Someone screamed in terror or triumph.

Without looking back, Noor broke into a run.

A red mist behind her and darkness in front. She lurched to the stairway and took them three at a time. On the ninth step she slipped and the crack of her butt landed on its edge. Such pain rocketed through her that she thought she'd fractured her spine. Scraping noises in the distance, then galloping. Whatever it was, it moved fast. One hand on her hip, teeth clenched, heart thundering in her ears, Noor glanced back.

Tabinda was at the first step, snorting, pawing at the bricks. She was on all fours. Her face was perfectly static, her forehead smooth. Not a fold, not a single crease, as if she were made from polished glass. Drool dangled in corkscrew threads from her chin.

As Noor watched, Tabinda lowered her head, sniffed the bricks stained with Noor's menstrual blood, and began to lap at them.

Noor turned and scuttled up the rest of the stairs. Pain chewed her ribs and back and hips, but she leapt blindly, not caring if she broke every bone in her body. Tabinda's smell behind her was acrid and meaty. It rushed at Noor. Noor vaulted across the last step and sprang toward the iron door.

Outside, the fog was a solid wall. Blind and barefoot, Noor slammed through it, using the brooding stupa as her only directional marker. Chips of glass and sharp pebbles stung her soles. Branches and what felt like bird bones crunched. Something bellowed behind her. A loud animal grunt. Noor clapped a hand over her mouth and kept running. She was wet and cold and trembling. Where was the fucking chopper? The night sky was silent. Her shalwar was soaked. She expected to crash face first into a wall any moment now. Instead, the sounds of the creature faded. Was it licking her blood trail at every step?

Weeping, Noor fled. The sharp bites of the alley became

hard ground. The fog thinned, showing her the school bus sprawled in the lot like a dead animal. She bounded toward it before remembering she didn't have the keys.

Noor wanted to scream, to slap her breasts and fall down, crying. She fought the impulse. Behind her the city was wailing. An earsplitting surreal ululation that bounced from wall to wall, door to door, and razored through her head. Lights bobbed in the corner of her eye. Spraying up dirt behind her, Noor sped past the vehicle, heading to the road winding out of the ruins.

The fog thickened again. Icy air knifed in and out of her lungs. When the sounds of the ruins died, she slowed to a trot. She was shaking all over and crying. Hot tears on frosted cheeks. Her feet were slippery with blood and stung in a hundred places. She had no idea where she was and the moon was dead somewhere. She was plodding through squelching mud now. Another step and her foot sank ankle deep. The wind whistled and picked up. Something rattled and she flinched. Pattering of feet or clomping of hooves? Terror washed over her. She yanked out her foot, lunged and landed in gelid water. Something slithered over her foot. A shower of water plumed over her when she struggled upright, tripped and nearly fell.

A misshapen root wide as her arm. She was at the riverbank. Had she once thought its smell rotten? It was mossy and sweet. The Sind River gurgled and babbled. Malformed cypress knees poked out of the fog like gravestones. Ghost acacia and lilacs swayed above her, their cocooned branches rustling. Glinting eyes speckled the webs. They undulated and disappeared as she splashed through the tree line. The fog curtain was so dense she could wrap it around herself and disappear forever.

A figure bobbed ahead in the trees. A flash of light that ignited the mist briefly and was gone. Noor's eyes widened. Part of her wanted to turn and bolt, but what if it was the Army come to find them? With utmost care she lifted the cuffs of her shalwar and tiptoed through the water. Curls of dark moss like a woman's hair floated between her legs, which gleamed with congealed blood. The cypress knees were more numerous here. They protruded in various geometric shapes.

One was almost like a little stool.

Her sight rippled, but not before she saw the figure crouching in the foliage. It was very tall and angular and seemed to perch on or by a poplar trunk. It wore something around its head, which could have been a headdress or a shawl.

Hamid! The bus driver. It had to be him. Dear God, let it be him. Noor choked back a sob and sloshed through mist and river water toward the silent figure riding the trees.

AFTERWORD

My friend, a well-regarded short fiction editor, hates writing introductions to her anthologies. She believes her choice of stories has more to say about her than she does. It is an honorable position: our works should be better than us, last longer than us, should not be defined by us.

I, however, enjoy a glimpse of the author's silhouette in the window of their art.

Midnight Doorways: Stories, originally subtitled *Fables from Pakistan*, is a collection of seven pieces from my first decade of professional writing, which began in 2013. The raison d'être for these fictions is the same as the reason for the original subtitle: these are *fables* from *Pakistan.* If 'fable' is defined as an outlandish lie that narrates a useful truth, the ultimate truth of these stories is that they are dreams from a disjointed, haunted country. Like the metaphysicians of Borges's mythical Tlön, I may have sought astonishment rather than exactitude in my chosen mode of storytelling, but, then, we live with exacting reality every day and either, untempered by dream or hope, eventually may prove overwhelming

For the longest time I battled with the question of genre for these stories. Not because 'genre' is a dirty word – I could give two hoots about that – but because as a teen I gravitated to horror and dark fiction and assumed I'd want to only write that. Over time, I've reluctantly come to conclude that I'm more interested in history, myth, and fable, how they interdigitate in all sorts of uncanny and, yes, horrific ways than in sending shivers down your spine. I'm fascinated by hidden histories, malformed love, science and scientific metaphors, and the secret lives of ghosts. I have little understanding but harbor tremendous fondness for poetry, especially the verses of Ghalib, Iqbal, Rumi, Sahir, Faiz Ahmed Faiz and Ahmad Fraz that I grew up with. While I have lost a fair chunk of my Urdu vocabulary since my school days, I continue to be moved to melancholia and saudade when I listen to a ghazal. Such influences have inevitably taken root in my work.

In an essay in *Dawn*, Aamer Hussein called me 'the fabulist of Lahore'. I think the writer of these stories *is* a fabulist; he's also a charlatan, a troubadour and a teller of tall tales. At varying times he labels himself a writer of science or speculative fiction before quickly changing gears to claim horror as his own, then discards both when the moment suits him. His plans remain nefarious: he aims to slip the truth of the human condition past your preconceived barricades of logic.

Wonder tales, like poetry, live in the bone marrow of South Asia. They hide in our scriptures, prance about in our epics, qissas and cautionary literature. You can hardly visit the mosque or temple without hearing of miracles and magic. At the heart of a wonder tale is a sense of awe at the vastness of the universe and the smallness of human life. One *will* inevitably miss most of it; hence the longing to apprehend the magical and the divine.

If realist literature looks for the extraordinary in the ordinary, fables or wonder tales look for the ordinary in the extraordinary, and bring it home.

At times I've been asked about the connective tissue binding these stories. While previously I'd have said there is no singular thematic thread, lately I'm convinced these are ghost stories. And if every love story is a ghost story, as David Foster Wallace once wrote to his mentor Richard Elman (Wallace himself a fan of Borges' fantastic fictions), it stands that every ghost story is also a love story.

Love, ghosts and wonders, then. If that's the meat and bones of this book once the skin is parted, dear reader, I'll be pleased to accept your savouring it so.

— Usman T. Malik
14 January 2022
Lahore

PUBLICATION HISTORY

'Ishq' – *Black Static* 43, November 2014
'The Wandering City' – *Us in Flux*, July 2020
'Resurrection Points' – *Strange Horizons*, August 2014
'The Fortune of Sparrows' – *Black Feathers*, February 2017
'Dead Lovers On Each Blade, Hung' – *Nightmare Magazine*, November 2018
'The Vaporization Enthalpy of a Peculiar Pakistani Family' – *Qualias Nous*, August 2014
'In the Ruins of Mohenjo-Daro' – *The Mammoth Book of Cthulhu*, April 2016

ACKNOWLEDGEMENTS

I am in debt to the editors who originally acquired these stories and provided valuable feedback: John Joseph Adams, Michael Bailey, Bob Beard, Andy Cox, Ellen Datlow, Joey Eschrich, Paula Guran, Brit Mandelo, An Owomoyela and Julia Rios.

My sincerest gratitude to the wonderful littérateurs who read the first draft of this collection and allowed me to quote their reactions.

I'm indebted to Musharraf Ali Farooqi and Aamer Hussein without whose support this publication might well have been deferred for another few years.

My gratitude to the Clarion West Writers Workshop; my Clarion West instructors, Elizabeth Hand, Neil Gaiman, Joe Hill, Margo Lanagan, Samuel R. Delany and Ellen Datlow, and the wonderful writers at Clarion West who read the seeds of these stories and gave valuable feedback: Helena Bell, John Costello, Geetanjali Dighe, David Edison, Fabio Fernandes, Jennifer Giesbrecht, Vince Haig, Nicole Idar, Alex Kane, Liam Meilleur, Shannon Peavey,

Nick Saelstrom, Kelly Sandoval, Allison Solano, Hugo Xiong, Neon Yang and E. Lily Yu.

Special thanks to my very patient agent Markus Hoffmann; editor-critic Tarun Saint who has been an early supporter of my work; and the editorial team at Hachette India, including Poulomi Chatterjee who acquired the book, Swarnima Narayan who worked closely with me throughout the publication process and Harshad Marathe for the lovely cover.